PRAISE FOR
Red Carpet Rivals

Red Carpet Rivals is to the movies what *The Devil Wears Prada* is to fashion. *RCR* could have only been written by someone like Bobbi Kornblit who strolled down scores of red carpets with her husband, a movie executive. With humor, a little snark, an eye for glamour, and an ear for understanding the real Hollywood, Kornblit weaves an intriguing tale behind the glitz.

—Mickey Goodman,
Author/Journalist/Ghostwriter

An absolutely delightful read. Bobbi Kornblit digs into her years as a Hollywood insider and delivers a very funny, irreverent, and mischievously shocking tale of what really goes on behind the scenes in the film industry. Her characters jump off the page and into your head and heart.

—Steve Coulter,
Actor/Writer, *House of Cards* &
The Walking Dead

Ever wondered what it was like to walk the red carpet in Hollywood? Get out a glass of champagne because here's your chance! Bobbi Kornblit gives us an insider view into the glamorous lives of movie studio moguls and actors in her new *Red Carpet Rivals*. Fast pacing, unexpected plot twists, delicious rivalries, and poignant love stories are all wrapped into a novel that will keep you reading well into the night. Move over, Jackie Collins!

—Kellie Coates Gilbert,
Author of the engaging and popular
Sun Valley Series

Glamorous rivals look for love onscreen and off in this fast-paced tale about Hollywood. Surprising relationships surface in this wickedly funny, sexy novel that dishes about the movie studios and the stars.

—Julie Spira,
Bestselling Author,
The Perils of Cyber-Dating

Strap yourself in for a wild and funny ride into the world that exists behind Hollywood's publicity glitz and talk-show chatter. A wickedly gleeful page-turner of a book.

—Mike Rose,
Author of *Lives the Boundary* and
The Mind at Work

Bobbi Kornblit's characters are so rich and her story so beautifully nuanced that I forget that I am actually reading. Wherever the characters are, I am there with them—listening, seeing, feeling.

—Fran Burst,
Director/Producer,
The Twelve Lives of Sissy Carlyle

Red Carpet Rivals takes us behind the scenes of the privileged, pampered, decadent worlds of Hollywood's Beautiful People. Each chapter gives us a private, VIP tour peering into a secret close-up of both historic Hollywood as well as that of today's glitz and glam and backstabbing smarm. What happens behind those gilded closed doors and cloistered movie sets? Who are the lovers and haters behind those sparkling veneer grins? What's "reel" and what's "real"? Once you step onto this unrivaled red carpet journey the answers will definitely surprise you.

—Cara Wilson-Granat,
Author/Storyteller/
Inspirational Speaker

Glitz, glamour, romance, friendship, betrayal, sexual harassment, private ambitions and publicity stunts—it's all in there! *Red Carpet Rivals* is a stimulating and entertaining romp through relationships and events leading up to Hollywood's biggest event of the year. Award-winning author Bobbi Kornblit pulls from her own real-life experience in her second novel. You'll really enjoy this walk down the red carpet knowing that her involvement with the movie industry gives authenticity and insider knowledge. I loved it and I know you will, too!

—Myra McElhaney,
Author, *Building A Life You Love After*
Losing The Love of Your Life

Red Carpet
Rivals

Red Carpet Rivals

BOBBI KORNBLIT

BAK LOT PRESS

BAK LOT
PRESS

www.RedCarpetRivals.com

In loving memory of
Simon Kornblit,
My leading man.

Fasten your seats belts. It's going to be a bumpy night!

—Bette Davis
as Margo Channing
All About Eve, 1950

PROLOGUE

"Password Rejected" glowed on the computer screen. Preston Cooper slammed his fist on the desk and then slowly retyped his personal access code for the online ballot for the Movie Constellation Awards: 1stConstance4Coop!

"If this happens one more damn time, I'll be shut out of the system and will miss the deadline. Voting online is harder than hacking into the Pentagon. At least I can remember my password, but the letters don't show up when I type!" he muttered. "Do me a favor—make the sign of the cross."

His valet, Peter Trent-Jones, touched his forehead and then swept his hand in quick little circles.

"Oh, you think I'm crazy?" Scrolling down the acting category, Preston Cooper delighted at the sight of each letter of his full given name. "Success!"

He was usually referred to as "Coop" around Hollywood insiders and in the tabloids. He savored the proof of his acting chops, printed in bold letters next to his starring role in *Big House, Little Lady*, an update of Jack London's 1916 novel, *The Little Lady of the Big House*. Coop decisively marked the slot for Lead Actor. He surveyed the room, imagining where he would display the golden statuette of a woman reaching for a star, the Constance Award.

"Too bad I chose to go online instead of filling out a paper ballot. I'd get a pen mounted for the historic occasion if I won—just like the president signing a treaty," Coop said.

"And what war are we fighting these days?" Peter Trent-Jones inquired.

"The Battle of Sirena! Like always, with my ex-wife, 'the plaintiff.'"

He chose "Paula's Love Dilemma" from *Big House, Little Lady* for Best Song. Coop followed the urge to pick every award for which his movie was nominated, representing his true feelings—that the flick was a kick-ass piece of filmmaking.

"No problem figuring out the acting awards, but what the hell's the difference between Best Sound and Sound Editing? Do me a favor and find the descriptions." Coop tossed Trent-Jones the pamphlet of rules the Movie Constellation Association provided to its nearly four thousand members.

The valet dutifully flipped through the booklet. "It says here that Sound Editing ..."

"Oh, never mind. *Big House* is going to crush the competition." Coop continued filling in his choices at a rapid pace. Then he rested his mouse and pinched the bridge of his nose, slowly reading the list of the five nominees for Lead Actress. "Rosita Lupe Paloma—hilarious. Tiffany Channing can't make a bad picture, and she's going for an even dozen Constance Awards."

"She's always a front-runner. The woman is an absolute chameleon," Trent-Jones agreed.

"Fourteen-year-old Arizona Fields is just too damn young to win. Kerri Lang—playing a maid has always fared well with the voters."

"A noble profession," Trent-Jones said while straightening a stack of scripts on the ornate desk.

Coop softly uttered, "And then there's Sirena." He held his head in his hands, thinking of the past. Costarring in *Big House, Little Lady* with Sirena Jackson, when they were married, had seemed like a dream.

Coop wondered, *When did working with Sirena turn into the worst nightmare of my life?*

1

COOP

W HEN PRESTON COOPER WALKED INTO A ROOM, women looked up from their cocktails, heads turned, and even men stole glances of the hottest leading man in Hollywood. Tall, blond, and ripped, he seemed bigger than life—particularly on-screen.

And that smile made women melt.

The Movie Constellation Association gave Coop the nod when he made the cut to be listed as part of the stable of five greats who were nominated as Lead Actor in a Motion Picture, which made him feel he had "arrived." He was recognized for his strengths as an actor and not just for his stellar looks.

On the long-awaited day of the awards ceremony, rows of klieg lights were readied in position to sweep the night sky to announce the Movie Constellation Awards: the premier ritual in Southern California that consumes the City of Angels. The question of the day would soon be answered: Who would win a Constance Award, the most coveted prize in cinema?

At half past three, a dark sedan snaked up a palm-lined driveway past a pair of majestic marble lions and then idled on the automobile court of an Italianate villa in Bel Air, Lion's Lair, the home of Preston Cooper.

The housekeeper, Leticia, parted the silk drapes puddled on the polished floor to get a better look at the vehicle parked out front. Sunlight spilled into the room, illuminating the fur of Harlow, the snow-white Turkish Angora cat perched on the windowsill. "*Gatito*, no fancy stretch, just a big black car. *Dios mio*," she said, shaking her head.

She pushed the elevator button and then wiped it with the corner of her crisp white apron. The shaft remained quiet—on the blink again. She mused how *Señora* Sirena used to demand perfection and never missed an opportunity to rule over the household staff. Leticia was glad that it was now *her* role to run things as she saw fit since there was no "woman of the house" at home anymore.

She trudged to the top of the staircase and knocked softly on a door etched with a pair of lions in the center panel. Conversations drifted from beneath the threshold, a mixture of several steadily rising voices. She knocked softly and pressed her cheek against the door. "*Señor* Cooper, your ride, he is here. What I should tell the driver?"

The crystal knob rotated, and then a woman's hand fluttered through an opening in the doorway. Coop's publicist, Francine Darten, barked, "Mr. Cooper won't be ready for at least another hour." The sharp words sliced the air. "Tell him he's fucking early and to cool his jets!" Harlow darted into the room seconds before the entry to the inner sanctum slammed shut, the door just missing her elegant, long tail.

"*Si, Señorita* Darten, I tell him." Leticia marched down the stairs, paused for a beat, and then headed back to the kitchen. She decided to wait until the doorbell rang, and then she'd deliver the news. She thought, *Jets? What jets? The driver gets more money the longer he waits—no problema.*

Inside the upstairs bedroom, Preston Cooper draped his shirtless, lanky frame onto a chaise. The cat pounced next to him, seductively nestling, eager to have her neck rubbed.

Coop's entourage—his publicist, hairdresser, and valet—scurried around like a swarm of bees set in motion. He stroked Harlow until he heard her throaty purr and then picked up a free weight to get in a few reps. His muscles flexed and stretched like a powerful wave, a force of nature.

Standing behind him, Stefano Bernini, the reigning hairstylist to the stars, ran his hands through Coop's famous blond locks. Stefano checked to see if any dark roots had sprouted in the flaxen field. "Still looks good enough for a close-up," Stefano said. "Backlit, you'll be Adonis incarnate—or like Robert Redford in *The Natural*."

"Stef, just cut it, goddammit!" Francine commanded. "Coop looks like a homeless man from the mission—not the world's biggest box office star on Movie Constellation Awards night."

Stefano narrowed his eyes at Francine. "The darker roots give character and look more natural. Trust me."

"He needs color!" Francine said.

Stefano paused with his brush held in midair. "Francine, how about loosening your grip on my balls? I thought you were a publicist—not an artiste. Julia didn't give me a hard time when I did her this morning." He spoke without looking up, still toying with Coop's stringy strands that swept into his intense blue eyes.

"Settle down, kids. Hey, anything to do with my head—or just plain getting head—*is* my business," Coop said in mock disdain that instantly morphed into a dazzling smile. "Not to worry, ladies. And Stef, I'm really a lover, not a fighter."

"First Francine gives me a hard time and now you. I'm numero uno in this town, and people wait for months to see me," Stefano replied and stormed out of the room.

"Don't even think about Cannes this year, Stefano," Francine shouted loudly enough to carry down the sweeping staircase. "No more promenades on the Croisette for you, sweetheart." She kicked the door shut, her thin heel punching a pea-sized indent in the gleaming maple. "And never bite the hand that feeds you!" She turned to face Coop and puckered her thin red slash into a kiss.

Harlow emitted a low hiss in Francine's direction and flattened her ears. Then she rubbed her lush body against the leg of Coop's jeans, and he stroked her back.

Francine made a mental note to cross Stefano off the short list of stylists and makeup artists the studio would send to Cannes in the south of France in May. *Too bad*, she thought. *He's a pain in the ass, but he's a master cutter.*

Peter Trent-Jones emerged from the dressing room at the far side of the bedroom that rivaled royal boudoirs—with a rich purple velvet canopy in a crescendo over the bed. He examined the front of a sleek Italian tuxedo. "Master Preston, this dinner jacket looks as if it's been stuffed in the boot of an automobile," he said, wrinkling his nose.

"Peter, you always sound like an understudy practicing for Alfred Pennyworth in *Batman*," Francine taunted.

Coop flashed Francine a quick conspiratorial grin, signaling it was time for them to lay off the teasing. She stuck out her tongue. Coop laughed and slowly ran his tongue across his upper lip in an exaggerated mock sensual response.

Coop's fashion stylist had selected a notch-lapel tux and made sure it was delivered at noon by a special courier who had hand-carried the tuxedo on the flight from Milan to Los Angeles; the box had occupied a first-class seat. When Coop was asked on the red carpet, "Who are you wearing?" he'd be able to give an A-lister's answer.

Francine picked up the red bow tie that was laid out on the bed and tossed it to Coop. As he snatched it out of the air, her eyes followed his well-toned body, which reminded her of a walking anatomy chart.

Fighting the urge to stare, she involuntarily responded to the star's sexy charm, along with an underlying intensity Preston Cooper exuded without really trying. "None of that stuffy your-father's-black-tie-look for you. The tabloids will have a field day with your nod to the red carpet with your neckwear. You'll look very hot!" she said, thinking how she wouldn't mind a few minutes alone with him on that big bed now that Coop was single again and Sirena was completely out of his personal life.

"They'll crucify me in the tabloids if I walk onstage in this gawd-awful red. Think it's on target?" he asked, playing a game of toss with the tie. Harlow's celadon eyes followed the flying strip of fabric as if she were stalking an unsuspecting cardinal, ready to pounce at any minute.

"Who cares what they say as long as they spell Cooper with a C and your face is plastered on every magazine cover. Hey, your hair is too long." Francine tousled his shaggy mane. "Hell, I'd have you wear a T-shirt at the Constance Awards if it'd grab more ink!" she said, chewing on the tip of her glasses.

Trent-Jones snatched the tie in midair and placed it next to the crisp white dress shirt.

Francine paced the room like a drill sergeant. Her high heels halted abruptly in front of Coop. She drew her index finger to her lips and cupped her chin while she took a long, appraising look. "If you're not going to cut that hair, then slick it back. Just get that shit out of your eyes!"

"Okay, already. You're worse than my ex was, always busting my chops. When's Sirena going to arrive at the Movie Constellation Awards? I want to get to the theater first to make a grand entrance before she does."

"The minute she's a block away from the entrance, Charlie Wallach from Silverlake Pictures swore she'd alert us. Sirena's limo driver will tip us off about her every move. Charlie promised him a walk-on in your next action flick in exchange for the info," Francine said, treading back and forth again, gnawing at her ragged nail until it drew blood. "Since Sirena's up for a Lead Actress award, I'm sure she'll stretch out her time on the red carpet for as long as she possibly can. I can assure you that you'll beat your ex-wife—I mean, you'll get there first."

Francine had arrived at Coop's mansion, Lion's Lair, dressed for the evening's awards festivities in a sleek black evening gown. If she was in photographs standing near her clients, she would appear as a VIP guest and not a working professional.

As a publicist, she knew her role was to be the power behind the stars, a gatekeeper—not the center of attention. She was never without the diamond star pendant on a platinum chain hanging around her neck.

Years ago at the first sign of his success in the movies, Coop, her favorite and most famous client, had bestowed it as a personal thank-you gift. In addition to her hefty fee for her work publicizing *Best Boy*—his first film that broke one hundred million at the box office—the studio's marketing department had footed the five-thousand-dollar tab for the jewelry from Tiffany's, adding it to the picture budget, along with her salary.

Francine's red-soled stiletto heels were her trademark. Even though she led a cadre of young acolytes eager to do her bidding, the head publicist always guarded the A-listers for herself.

The opening bars of the "Entertainment Tonight" theme song chimed on her cell. Francine pushed her blunt chestnut hair, highlighted with two bold, frosted blond streaks, behind her ears and took the call. She relayed the message to Coop. "Charlie says she'll meet us on the red carpet in front of the theater." She hung up and said,

"Okay, sweetheart, chop-chop. Finish getting dressed and get your royal Hollywood ass in gear." She patted Coop on his tight bottom.

"Terribly cheeky, Miss Darten," Trent-Jones chided while scurrying around collecting the shirt and tuxedo jacket.

Francine flashed him her throbbing, ragged middle finger and then wiggled the rest. "Cheerio, ta-ta, ol' boy, or whatever it is you say in your native tongue in Kansas." She fixed on Coop's sparkling blue eyes that caught the glint of the chandelier above the bed. "You're ready for your close-up, Mr. Cooper."

Coop unleashed his multimillion-dollar smile and shooed Harlow off the chaise. He dropped his jeans and grabbed his tuxedo pants, sliding them over his impossibly long legs.

Francine stood riveted, never taking her eyes off him.

"Shirt!" he commanded.

Trent-Jones held out the starched white sleeves into which a pair of golden biceps disappeared. He artfully positioned the red bow tie.

Coop tucked in his shirt and zipped to a full audience.

"Your dinner jacket, *suh*." With a silver monogrammed brush, the valet dusted the wide shoulders of the tuxedo, sending a few long white cat hairs flying.

Reflected in the kaleidoscope of glistening facets in the Venetian cut glass mirror, Preston Cooper stroked his lapel and rewarded himself with a satisfied wink. He cleared his throat and said, "Members of the Movie Constellation Assoc—" His lips widened into a forced smile to check his teeth and then announced, "It's showtime!"

2
CHARLIE

CHARLIE WALLACH'S EARPIECE FIT NEATLY against her simple diamond studs. She tightly drew in her arms, trying to fend off the incessant rain. "Why the hell did they change the Movie Constellation Awards to February? It's too damn cold in 'sunny Southern California,'" she grumbled.

Her assistant, Gabe Ashton, glanced up from his clipboard. He brushed a lock of jet-black hair out of his piercing blue eyes, which were obscured by Clark Kent-style glasses with heavy frames. His beard was closely trimmed to trendy stubble.

Charlie glanced at him, thinking his twentysomething face with imperfect features came together in a pleasing way. She had recommended Gabe for hiring although he applied with experience from another industry. He had been an assistant brand manager at a manufacturer of personal care products, specializing in the deodorant division. He said that he wanted to get out of the armpit of marketing and could apply his skills in a more exciting category: the movie business. He also was willing to take a pay cut to work at the film studio.

Gabe continued to study the schedule for the red carpet arrivals at the Movie Constellation Awards ceremony. "What's the dealio?" he asked. "Whose brilliant idea was it to hold this shindig now instead of at the beginning of April?"

"I'm freezing my ass off, and I'm not even that airhead starlet over there who's running around in a backless gown," Charlie said.

Gabe removed his jacket and draped it around her shoulders. "I read somewhere in the trades that they did it to avoid sports playoffs and to get the nominations in before the other awards shows swayed the Movie Constellation members' votes," he said.

"Well, nobody thought about how we're going to launch the awards marketing campaigns while we're trying to get our December picture releases off the ground." Charlie, Vice President of Marketing Products at Silverlake Pictures, felt like she had been working on fast forward like a Keystone Cop for the past two months, ever since the nomination ballots were available to the voting members of the Movie Constellation Association.

She edged away from the leaky awning that covered the red carpet winding its way from the curb to the doors of the theater in West Hollywood. "My outfit's going to be history by the time I make it to my seat! Look at these water spots. Your jacket's not much better," she complained to Gabe. Then Charlie considered the quality of their seats in the loge, high above the main floor action—wondering if she'd ever be considered important enough to sit in the orchestra section, jockeying for armrest space with the nominees. "Nobody's going to see us in the nosebleed section, so why should I give a damn?"

"It's bad enough that members of our marketing department had to fork over the tickets they got in the Constance Awards lottery. Screw those self-centered actors! Just because Brent Wilder is up for Featured Actor, he thinks he can bring his girlfriend, his yoga coach, *and* his daughter," Gabe said. To fight the creeping dampness, he stomped his feet on the soggy carpet, leaving dark crimson shoeprints.

"Heaven forbid he'd be satisfied with the two tickets he gets as a nominee. If I'm sitting in these shitty seats next year, I swear I'll quit!" Charlie fumed.

"Hey, at least we're not watching it at home like most of the marketing department. One day, I hope I get a pair of prime seats for the Constance Awards on the main level. There's a consolation for this year—our table is in a sweet spot at the Constellation Ball, not far from the band."

Charlie squeezed his arm and smiled. "You're still a little green, but that's part of your boyish charm."

"Thanks for the vote of confidence," he said with a crooked smile while opening his umbrella and moving closer to shield her from the leaks.

An infinite line of black limos pulled up to the curb. Cameras flashed and searing television lights lined the walkway, sparkling like the crystal trims on evening gowns. The "bleacher bunch"—die-hard fans who had won the lottery for the coveted seats on rows of metal risers near the limo drop-off area—cheered the arrivals. They remained dry in the downpour because the event organizers had erected a canopy to shield them from the inclement weather, an improvement after years of being left unprotected in the elements.

In a secondary traffic arrival lane, attendees who had driven their own cars and had hiked from the outlying parking lots in the hinterlands were ushered through a security tent. They were herded into lines to pass through metal detectors. Women's jewelry triggered the alarms, and they spread-eagled for wand searches, as best they could manage in their form-fitting gowns, often with deep slits. Cameras and cell phones were confiscated by the guards and could be redeemed after the ceremony. Photographs by nonprofessionals were strictly verboten. The A-list celebrities, considered terrorist-proof, were exempt from being inconvenienced by the annoying screenings.

Silverlake Pictures brought its own security team to watch over its stable of stars. Jamaal Kenter, in his tux with a black satin bulletproof vest, lingered on the edge of the arrival area. He whispered into the microphone clipped to his satin lapel, "The 'Raptor' hasn't landed yet." He continued to search the crowd, looking for his high-profile client, Coop.

Over the static buzzing in his ear, he heard Charlie's response. "He'd better get here soon. Any sign of 'Tweety Bird'?" Charlie started to pace, and Gabe struggled to keep up with her, holding the umbrella aloft.

"No clue where Sirena ... I mean, 'Tweety' is," Jamaal's voice crackled.

"Keep me posted," Charlie said. The static abated.

Jamaal continually scanned the scene, searching for the unexpected among throngs of people who were all trying desperately to be noticed. He had never lost anyone under his watch and was determined there wasn't going to be a first time for disaster.

Across the walkway to the entrance to the theater, Charlie smoothed her hair, taming the damp tendrils that had escaped her dark chignon. *Where the hell is Coop?* she wondered.

The next limousine in line inched toward the designated drop-off spot in front of the theater. President of Marketing for Silverlake Pictures Arthur Fielgood and his wife, Teeni, stepped out of the stretch. Teeni deftly scooted to the edge of the limo seat and then contorted her hips to align with the door, avoiding an embarrassing flash. Refusing the helping hand of the white-gloved attendant, she smoothly emerged from the vehicle into the spotlight, wearing a custom-made magenta gown.

When first introduced to Arthur Fielgood, people often wondered if he was kidding about his last name. Although humorous, it proved to be an unforgettable moniker that had served him well when he was making his way up the corporate ladder in the motion picture business.

The constant strobe of camera flashes subsided. Sharon Roundtree from the *Movie Times Journal* pulled the Fielgoods aside for a quick photo op. Arthur wrapped his arm around his wife's petite shoulders, which were covered by a full-length mink coat.

"Make sure my coat doesn't end up looking like a drowned rat. This is *real* fur, not the faux crap that everyone else wears. Why isn't there someone who can hold an umbrella for us? This damn awning is leaking like a friggin' sieve, Artie," Teeni whined.

From the front row of a nearby bleacher, Teeni and Arthur heard a man shout, "Who the hell are they?"

Another fan replied, "Nobodies. Oh look—there's a real star getting out of that stretch! I hope that old couple gets out of the way so we can see the celebrities better."

Teeni stared ahead and advanced slowly. She plumped her lips into a closed-mouth smile, as she felt real smiles add wrinkles to the eyes and magnify the jowls. Arthur stopped to shake hands with anyone on the red carpet who seemed to recognize him.

The movie trades usually ran two-page spreads of Hollywood movers and shakers—the heads of studios and mini-mogul types. Arthur and Teeni were mainstays in the post-Movie Constellation Awards issues ever since he had been the head of Marketing at Silverlake. He had just signed a new contract for another five-year hitch.

In Hollywood, being a studio marketing president was like playing a high-stakes game of musical chairs. They rotated from one studio to another, depending on the current regime of the chairman of the motion picture division. It was a professional lineage of almost biblical proportions.

"Artie, stand over here," Teeni instructed. "You know I never like to be photographed from the left."

Arthur dutifully maneuvered to his wife's "good side."

"Last year you ran only a three-quarter shot of us in the paper; how about including my shoes this time? I'd better get some mileage out of this gown now because I can't wear it again once it's been in the press," Teeni said to the reporter, sounding like a neglected stepchild.

"Most are headshots, Mrs. Fielgood. It's really up to our photo editors to decide. I just write the words," Sharon replied, waving her pen and notebook in the air as proof.

"I'm counting on you to make my wife happy," Arthur whispered. "Scratch my back and I'll scratch yours."

From time to time, Sharon called Arthur for off-the-record quotes about stories when she hit a snag. In return, she always submitted his quotes from interviews for his approval before they ran in the issue—Hollywood's version of quid pro quo.

The photographer crouched in front of the couple. "Say 'brie!'"

When the shooter lowered his camera, a pair of ushers instantly appeared like special-effects genies guarding their magic carpet, flanking the Fielgoods. "Move along, folks. Keep the path clear for the celebrities."

Teeni's studied smile faded as she reluctantly sauntered to the outer edge of the crimson carpet with her husband. "One of these days you're going to be recognized by the general public."

Sharon shouted to the photographer, "Over there! Look who's standing on the award logo on the red carpet. Quick, let's grab a shot. 'Mr. Uberproducer's' cool, spiky hair is drooping from the rain. You've got to catch that!"

Arthur turned to Charlie near the arrival area and gave her a quick nod. Then he walked over and hugged her. "Wet enough for you, kiddo? All we need is a tsunami, and the evening will be complete. Let's just hope we get a landslide of wins with *Big House*."

"From your lips …" Charlie inched away from her boss.

Teeni tugged at Arthur's coat sleeve. "We're already late for the VIP reception. I'm sure everyone's wondering where we are."

As Charlie reached to shake the hand of her boss's wife, Teeni pulled back and then finally allowed Charlie to graze her limp fingertips. Teeni wasn't keen on human contact, even air kisses.

"Do you still enjoy going to the Movie Constellation Awards after all these years?" Charlie asked playfully.

"Yeah, a lot more fun than those poor schlubs who have to watch the ceremony on television," Teeni droned. "February is always the shittiest month. I used to spend most of it at our home on the Kona Coast in Hawaii. I'd love to be somewhere warmer, but I can't these days. You know my responsibilities with Arthur. We don't have any kids to divide my attention, and he needs me here at these events."

Approaching Arthur, the reporter said, "Let's try one more shot. My photographer checked his digital, and I want to make sure I've got a good one of the two of you."

"Sharon, send a few extra copies of the issue to Charlie, my marketing gal, won't you?" Arthur said.

Gabe watched the color drain from Charlie's cheeks after Arthur's disrespectful verbal demotion.

Sharon said, "Charlie, I'll get them to your assistant because I know you'll be up to your ears managing the post-awards madness tomorrow." She tried to help Charlie regain stature in front of Gabe.

The photographer snapped a few quick ones and checked his replay. "Got it!" he said and aimed at the next star emerging from the arrival lane.

Arthur eyed an usher headed his way. "See you inside, Charlie. Keep her in line, Gabe," Arthur said, followed by a laugh as rough as a nagging cough.

"Yes sir. Mrs. F, you look awesome," Gabe said.

Teeni cocked her head slightly toward Gabe but kept promenading with her arm tightly tucked into the crook of her husband's sleeve. They became engulfed in the line of glamorous women in glittery gowns and men in black tuxedos that moved at a snail's pace toward the festooned doors of the theater.

"You can unpucker your lips from Teeni's butt, Gabe," Charlie said and grabbed the umbrella.

Over the years, the Fielgoods had perfected the "red carpet shuffle," taking two steps forward and one step backward to prolong their time on the most famous walkway in the world. Cordoned off by red velvet stanchions, a row of gigantic golden Constance statues holding stars aloft glowed in the floodlights.

"His marketing gal, my ass," Charlie snapped. "I guess that's what they call vice presidents these days."

Gabe lightly squeezed Charlie's neck. She stroked his hand in appreciation of his support and then took a deep breath.

"I swear, in five more minutes I'm going inside whether Coop's here or not." Intermittent leaking raindrops plopped on Charlie's head—as frequently as her boss had sprinkled insults.

In front of the theater, the rain continued to bluster. The front awning sagged and groaned under the weight of the water. Celebrities cut short their precious time chatting on the red carpet with entertainment reporters for fear the canvas was going to collapse or their hairdos would fall.

Charlie forged her way to the front of the line to see if she could spot Coop's vehicle approaching. It was getting dangerously close to the final deadline for arrivals. She had told him that nominees and presenters had to take their seats no later than five o'clock, the drop-dead limit.

Drawing Gabe closer, she said, "I should have been with Coop on the ride over. I know all the tricks about getting here on time: Leave too early to beat the traffic and you miss the red carpet action; leave a few minutes too late and you're stuck in 'limo-land.'"

Gabe asked, "What's Coop's excuse for being late tonight?"

"You know he pushes everything to the limit: skydiving, race car driving. Why should this be different?" Charlie checked her watch and bit her lip. She wiped her brow, uncertain if her clamminess was from the rain or from her frayed nerves.

3
SIRENA

I N THE SEA OF BLACK LIMOS on the way to the Movie Constellation
Awards ceremony, a white stretch navigated like a posh ocean liner
cutting through the waves and exited from the Santa Monica Freeway.
Behind the black-tinted windows, Sirena Jackson lay flat with her
feet propped on the facing seat. Her toes, wrapped in shiny filaments
attached to silver spiked heels, pointed skyward toward the sunroof,
and a spray of diamonds dotted her sandal straps. Even the soles of
her shoes sparkled. The bugle beads on her dark blue gown glistened
like a starlit midnight sky.

Ethan Dean Traynor, the hottest young up-and-comer in
Tinseltown, stretched out next to Sirena. She mused how he literally
filled that bill as a "comer," erect and eager to please her night after
night. The blond surfer-dude type starred in the teen angst nighttime
soap, *The Zuma Beach Diaries*, the latest hit show by octogenarian
producer Abram Geller. Even though Ethan was in his twenties, he
played a seventeen-year-old who had ditched college to catch the curl
at Zuma Beach, north of Malibu.

Sirena, thirteen years his senior, was old enough to be cast as his mom. The tabloids continually compared Ethan to Coop, claiming an uncanny resemblance—both very Nordic with chiseled features.

"Hot stuff, you look awesome," Ethan said.

"Really? At first I didn't want to wear this old thing when my stylist, Geena, brought it to me. She finally convinced me that it's vintage, not just used clothing. She believes the Hollywood costumers of the past were the bomb."

Sirena's fashion consultant had plucked the rare Edith Head creation out of a vintage clothing shop on La Cienega Boulevard, lovingly restoring and saving it for the right client.

When Geena presented it to her, Sirena had protested, "No way I'm going to wear a recycled gown to the Movie Constellation Awards."

"They don't bead formals the way they used to or understand the way a garment should properly drape a real woman's body to display her assets. I wouldn't steer you wrong. You'll stand out in vintage," Geena had said as she smoothed the rows of iridescent beads.

The stylist had selected the dress to showcase Sirena's physical proportions that rivaled a classic Barbie doll: world-class breasts and a minuscule waist.

"I'm still not sure. How about a modern designer?" Sirena asked.

"With this gown, there's no chance of anyone else showing up with the same dress. You won't be featured in a magazine side by side in comparison with another celeb wearing your gown on Movie Constellation night. Slip it on."

Sirena shimmied into the gown. "Sold!" she said, dancing around, clutching the dress against her body.

In the limousine, Sirena tried not to bend in the middle so she wouldn't have a wrinkled midriff at the transparent lectern at the ceremony. Perched on the deep crevice of her cleavage, a famous jewel sparkled like a beacon in the dark—a 170-carat sapphire encircled by diamonds.

From the bank of seats in the rear of the elongated vehicle, stern-faced bodyguard Thomas Campbell kept a watchful eye on the borrowed bauble worth well over a million dollars. The manufacturer of her valuable jewel-encrusted high heels also benefited from the security. If this Cinderella were to lose her slipper at the end of the Constellation Ball, the insurance company would pay big-time.

The bodyguard sat next to Sirena's hair-and-makeup stylist, Amelia Patterson. The studio always hired her to accompany the fastidious actress whenever she had a public appearance. Amelia had made the trip to the French Riviera several times to keep Sirena's naturally platinum hair looking sleek and shiny. The star never went anywhere without Amelia, her best friend since childhood. She required that Amelia's services be written into her contracts along with the stipulation that Sirena's name appear above the title of the movie in all the promotional materials.

Sirena's flowing tresses looked as if they belonged to an angel on Earth, unlike the brittle, bottle-blonde celluloid goddesses of the past such as Jean Harlow and Marilyn Monroe. Not since Grace Kelly had there been an ice princess on the silver screen who melted the hearts of moviegoers—until Sirena Jackson.

People were fascinated with her catlike hazel eyes that morphed from green to brown, depending on the lighting and the skill of the photographers and cinematographers. She had sworn in countless interviews that she didn't enhance them with colored contact lenses.

Ethan leaned closer to Sirena in the limo.

"Sweetie, could you get your big gunboats away from my gown?" Sirena said, adjusting her train, which trailed onto the floor.

"Sorry, hot stuff. How 'bout a brewski?" He repositioned his size-twelve crocodile boots.

"Dang, I told them to stockpile a few magnums of champagne and some crystal flutes, but I forgot to get a kegger for you," she said, laughing.

She diverted her eyes from the small television screen tuned to the parade of stars entering the theater and gave her lover's aquiline nose a quick tweak on its bridge. She giggled when he swatted her hand away.

"Children, y'all play nice," Amelia chided. "Sirena, I'll have a little bubbly if you're going to open one of those bottles."

"For you, honey, anything. Thomas, how about popping Amelia's cork?" Sirena said.

"Very funny, just pass me the bottle and a couple of glasses, and I'll open it myself," Amelia said. Ethan sent the bottle to the back of the limousine. There was a loud pop and giggles from Sirena followed.

"Somebody pour me a glass," Sirena said. Amelia handed her a crystal flute without spilling any champagne on the gown. "Amelia, have some. You too, Thomas."

"I'll pass. I'm on duty," Thomas said.

"Me too," Amelia said. "Your hair has to look perfect on camera when you win!"

Sirena took a sip and focused her attention on the television screen, scanning the crowd of celebrities. In a close-up, entertainment correspondent Judy Simmons announced that everyone was anxiously waiting for the two biggest stars in Hollywood to arrive: Preston Cooper and Sirena Jackson—separately, of course.

"If we're in a battle for who's going to win their first Constance Award tonight, I've got another little game to play with my high-and-mighty ex; but first, I'm hungry," Sirena said.

She flipped a switch, and the opaque glass partition descended, revealing the limo driver. "And you are?" she asked, as if she were a queen speaking to one of her subjects.

"Max," the driver answered while looking at her in the rear-view mirror.

"Well, Max, keep your eyes on the road and hang a Louie."

"But the theater's straight ahead. Even though the traffic's a bear, this is the official route we're supposed to take. A lot of the side streets are blocked off." The cell phone in his breast pocket chimed. Max pulled it out and glanced at the caller ID. He whispered, "Yeah, it's me. We're on course, but something's happening. She wants to change the plan."

"What plan? Who's that?" Sirena asked. She sat up straight and let her train drop to the floor of the limo.

Max smacked his chewing gum a few times and then replied, "It's the main office."

"Okay, hand me the phone."

"Ma'am, can't do that."

"Then hang up the damn phone right now, or you'll never get another assignment from a major studio, I swear it!"

"Catch you in a few." Max ended his call.

"What's up? Coop put you up to something, didn't he?" Sirena probed.

"I don't know what you mean."

"You've got to be kidding! I'll give you a deal you can't refuse if you tell me what's going on."

"You mean I'll get a speaking part in a movie?" Max asked.

"No, buster, I mean you won't get fired in a New York minute."

"That's one heck of a deal. I'm supposed to make sure you get there a lot later than Mr. Cooper so he'll be able to take all the time he wants on the red carpet and not bump into you."

Sirena downed the last of her champagne and handed the empty glass to Ethan. He passed it to Thomas, who gave it to Amelia.

"Max, no more contact with your buddies until I tell you to," Sirena said, cupping her slender hand to her chin.

"Don't mess with your makeup!" Amelia shouted from the back of the car, clutching her cosmetics case on her lap.

"Now, Max, find out where *he* is right now!"

The driver phoned the dispatcher and learned that Coop was stuck in a massive bottleneck on the Santa Monica Freeway. He relayed the information to Sirena, who responded with a Cheshire Cat smile.

She said, "Listen to me loud and clear. We've got plenty of time. Make a left and pull into the Burger-Blast."

"Your wish is my command," the driver said, hoping he could change her mood and preserve his job.

She turned to Ethan and gave him an openmouthed movie kiss. He arched his body over hers, careful not to crush her gown.

"Your lipstick!" Amelia cried, watching her artful application get smudged.

"That's what you're here for," Sirena replied.

"Ethan, don't mess with her hair. I don't want to have to redo it in here!" Amelia chided.

"Amelia, hon, you can fix anything. That's why I can't be without you," Sirena cooed.

Amelia smiled and settled back in her seat.

The super-stretch pulled into the driveway of the burger joint. The limo glided forward and hugged the left side of the building. The crowd at Burger-Blast that was lined up well after lunchtime craned in unison to get a glimpse of the passengers hidden behind the tinted windows.

"Thomas, get me a hamburger with the works. Oh wait, tell them to hold the onions. How about the rest of y'all?" Sirena asked. "Sky's the limit."

"Thought we get dinner afterward at the Constellation Ball," Ethan said. "But you know me—I can always eat. Can I get a beer now?"

"Yeah, but it's going to be a root beer at this place. I've been starving myself to fit into this dress, but I think I'll faint onstage if I don't get something inside me right now."

Ethan gave her a knowing look. "That's what I'm here for."

"Sirena, skip the fries. All that seasoned salt will make your eyes puffy," Amelia said from the back. "Thomas, order me some of the guacamole. It's supergood."

Max cut the engine and brought the land boat to a stop.

"I'd much rather eat one of these burgers now because I can't wait several hours for the latest culinary creation at the Constellation Ball. I'll never make it until nine o'clock. I'd starve."

"I'm always hungry," Ethan said, nibbling at her lips.

"Let's really get some mileage out of this detour." Sirena punched a few numbers into her phone. "Everyone out! We're going inside to the counter." She sat upright and prepared to exit the limo, careful not to twist too much and dislodge any of the antique beads.

The driver scurried around the front of the massive car to assist her. The diner's sign reflected in a rainbow of oil-slicked puddles. Sirena gathered her train in both hands, draped it over her arm, and stepped gingerly onto the asphalt, careful not to douse her sparkling sandals in the pools of standing water. The passengers in the limo caught a lucky break in the rainfall.

The crowd of customers slowly drifted toward the white car. A handful of regulars were reluctant to forfeit their spots in line until they were sure it was worth the sacrifice. Teenage reconnaissance sorties began to swarm the limo.

A girl with a row of rings piercing her eyebrows screamed and bolted toward the stretch when Ethan emerged behind Sirena. In the next instant, she phoned a friend, shouting, "Oh my God, you're gonna think I'm trippin', but Sirena Jackson and Ethan Dean Traynor just showed up at Burger-Blast." The girl jumped up and down. "No, I'm not shitting you."

The rain had subsided into a soupy mist, turning the passing headlights into wide, glowing circles. The ominous afternoon skies looked like evening, with no sign of clearing up before the beginning of the Movie Constellation Awards ceremony.

Thomas ushered the stars directly to the front door of the diner, bypassing the maze of railing used to keep the customers in a queue, which was virtually empty because most were mobbing the two celebrities. The bodyguard feverishly flailed his bulging arms, trying to get some distance between the curious throngs and his famous charge and her valuable accessories. The masses pressed closer, and a girl snatched the hem of Sirena's train. Amelia yanked it free and gave the stunned teen a lethal look, maneuvering to stand as a shield in front of Sirena. A man in a Lakers jacket watched the ensuing pandemonium from his perch near the front door, smiling at his good fortune to have moved up in the line so quickly.

Once inside, a server hoisted a burger on a paper plate into Sirena's manicured hands. As Sirena sank her Chiclet-white teeth into the soft bun, cameras clicked in staccato, accompanied by a wave of blinding flashes. The paparazzi instantly materialized.

"Front page of major newspapers tomorrow, bet you a blow job," Sirena whispered to Ethan between bites, careful to smile for the paparazzi without revealing a morsel of hamburger in her mouth. She made a three-quarter turn to Ethan, away from the cameras, and ran her tongue along the tip of the oversized bun. "The headline had better not be 'Constance Award favorite bites big one.'"

"I'll bet that we'll both make the tabloids," Ethan said. He flashed her a devilish smile. "If you win, I promise you a very special surprise. Can we make a quick stop at the Pleasure Palace for a few adult toys? It's pretty close to here."

"Not now, sweetie. Sounds like either way I win," she said, laughing. "Okay, everybody back in the car! It's showtime!"

Sirena handed her uneaten burger to Thomas, who was never more than six inches away from the bejeweled necklace and shoes. The bodyguard clutched the plate in his muscular hands and pursed his lips in a frown. "But we didn't get our food yet," he said. In a moment of weakness, he considered stuffing the rest of her burger in his mouth but then reluctantly shoved it into the trash barrel.

"Thomas, if I win an award tonight, I'll buy you a dozen hamburgers tomorrow!" Sirena said. She strolled toward the door, looking at a wall of autographed celebrity headshots. Like a Hollywood stamp of approval, black-and-white glossies of stars shared wall space with the mayor of Los Angeles.

Above the buzz, an elderly customer with a mouthful of burger said, "Hey, doll, you're so pretty you ought to be up on that wall too."

"Thanks. I'll send them a photo tomorrow, and I'll sign it with a red lipstick kiss," Sirena said.

The man responded with his most beguiling snaggletoothed grin.

"Amelia, come on. You don't need to eat this stuff. You'll blow up like a balloon, and then you'll never be able to fit into my old clothes," Sirena said, grabbing Amelia's hand.

"Thanks for always thinking of me," Amelia muttered with a crooked smile.

"I always do," Sirena said, giving her friend's hand a squeeze.

Within two minutes, the white limo was back on the road. The mist had escalated into a driving rain, and the windshield wipers beat out a steady rhythm. Max deftly wove the stretch between cars, darting onto side streets and alleys, gaining blocks at a time when he resurfaced on the main road.

"Find out where *he* is," Sirena said to Max.

"But I'm not sure I can."

"Just do it and stick yourself right in front of Coop's car. I don't care how, but make it happen! Not another word." She slid the glass partition closed, ending the conversation like an exclamation mark.

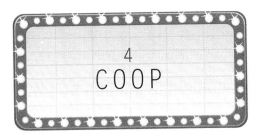

4
COOP

RAIN CLOUDS LOOMED OVER LOS ANGELES during the day of the awards, with a shower replacing the overhanging smog.

"What the fuck? That white limo almost rammed into us on the turn when it cut in front. What's with that?" Coop shouted.

"Beats me, sir. People are doin' some crazy-ass driving in this wet weather. You know Californians can't drive in the rain. We're just about there."

"It's getting close to airtime. The producer's going to bust a gut if we don't meet his production schedule for the telecast," Francine said.

"Game's up! I don't care where Sirena is. We're so late now that I'd better have my feet on that red carpet in about two minutes, or there's going to be some serious hell to pay," Coop warned. "This is my lucky night, and my ex-wife is not going to screw it up!"

"I'll get Charlie on the line. If we're stuck much longer, we might end up stalled like those poor bastards," Francine said. She pointed toward a limo with its hood raised, sidelined along the curb. "Maybe we should offer them some Grey Poupon, like in the old commercial." She tried to douse Coop's fuse that was burning down furiously.

"Yeah, remember on my first nomination for *Red-Hot, Skin Deep* when we were stranded on the freeway on a median? I thought Sirena was going to go crazy standing out there on the shoulder with the wind whipping up dust from the passing trucks and cars. Finally another limo stopped, figuring we were headed for the Movie Constellation Awards ceremony since who else would be stranded on the interstate in a tux in the middle of the afternoon? It was a miracle, but they stopped to pick us up."

"I guess freeway hitchhiking mass murderers don't usually wear tuxedos. You live right, sweetheart." Francine gave his thigh a playful squeeze.

"A little higher, Ms. Darten," he laughed, showing his megawatt smile.

Francine giggled and slowly removed her hand from his leg. She stroked her diamond star necklace.

"Our limo driver had told us someone from his service would come rescue us in their own ride because there wasn't another limousine to be had in all of Southern California and most of Nevada," Coop said. "Can you imagine my showing up in a regular car? Being in this sedan tonight and not in a stretch limo is bad enough. Did I ever tell you that our Good Samaritan was Luther Jackson Jr.'s daughter, who was going to the ceremony because her dad was getting a special posthumous tribute?"

"Talk about luck! After that, Silverlake Pictures switched car services. That screw-up cost the limo company big bucks!" Francine said.

"Sirena was furious. On her first trip to the Constance Awards, she didn't want to look like she'd been selling oranges on a freeway ramp. Good thing the 'bed head' was popular that year. I was the one who was up for the award—not her—but all she ever cared about was herself and how she looked."

"Yes, she pitched a fit when her place card at the Constellation Ball said Mrs. Preston Cooper instead of Ms. Sirena Jackson. She almost wouldn't sit down at the table until that card was replaced," Francine said.

"I can give you several million reasons why there's no chance her name card will say Mrs. Preston Cooper this year!" Coop said.

5

COOP

THE MEMBERS OF THE MOVIE Constellation Association started taking Preston Cooper seriously as an actor of considerable talent when he had landed a role that made the leap from a teen heartthrob to a celluloid contender. He caught their attention by playing a part that was a surefire way to get a nod: portraying a person with a disability that overshadowed the focus on his astounding good looks. In *Red-Hot, Skin Deep*, Coop starred as a rookie fireman who was burned over seventy percent of his body while saving a family of civil rights activists from a church torched by the Klan. It was a sizable stretch from his usual pretty-boy roles, but it didn't garner him the big prize—only a nomination. He got the Mississippi accent down pat since it had some similarities to his native Texan drawl that he had previously worked so diligently to eradicate. Competitor Ricardo Perrino walked away with another Constance Award to add to his collection, playing a deaf and blind mountain climber who overcame insurmountable odds to conquer Mount Everest.

It was a far cry from the days when Robert Preston Cooper arrived in Hollywood in his rickety old car with the four thousand dollars his grandfather had left him after passing away at ninety-three in Bent Branch, Texas.

Robby Cooper, as he was known in high school, couldn't make his way through a math equation, but he had an uncanny ability to memorize material by rote. He struggled with constant fatigue and muscle weakness, and to the shame of his football coach father, he couldn't make the team. His dad, Rowdy Cooper, insisted he attend all the practices and appointed him manager, a title that made the boy an even larger target for ridicule among the school jocks.

Mr. Elkins, the drama coach, saw potential in the young man with good looks and an excellent memory. The teacher, a stumpy man in his thirties with skin as pale as parchment, stayed late to work with his star student after football practice was over.

One afternoon Mr. Elkins asked, "Robby, have you thought about a stage name?"

"What's wrong with my own name, Mr. E? Robert Preston Cooper. I think it sounds pretty good."

"For one thing, there's already an actor named Robert Preston. Ever heard of *The Music Man*?"

"Oh, yeah, but he's old. Must be about forty." Robby picked up a piece of chalk from the blackboard. The letters he scribbled squeaked across the dull green surface. "P-R-E... Preston Cooper. I never heard of a star named Preston."

"It's got a ring of old Hollywood: Gary Cooper—even Elvis Presley. Robby, I've got a strong hunch you're going to make it." Mr. Elkins started to erase the letters but lingered for a moment before the name disappeared.

"Ya think so?"

"You might be like some of the movie greats. But you'd better get some dance training along the way. It could help you with your coordination."

Robby stumbled, banging into the leg of Dr. Elkins's desk. "That's just what I need—something else for the guys to razz me about."

Robby's dad, Rowdy Cooper, swore he had burnt-orange blood coursing through his veins. The only place he wanted his son to go to college was the University of Texas at Austin. He knew in his heart that Robby didn't have the grades and would never land an athletic scholarship. Football had always been the main focus of the Cooper household.

As a young boy, Robby had developed slowly. Jocelyn had noticed that her beautiful golden-haired boy struggled to grasp small items such as jacks and miniature plastic soldiers. Rowdy said he needed something better to hang onto—a miniature football. In the afternoons while Coach was still at practice, Jocelyn lined up pennies, thimbles, thread, cotton balls, and any little items she could find to play a game of "pick up the prize" with her four-year-old son. Sometimes a tiny object would stubbornly elude his grip like it was glued to the table. She urged him to try again, working daily to improve his dexterity.

At dinner, Robby's head tilted to one side, as if tired from holding up its weight. Jocelyn tapped his shoulders. "Straighten up, son. Don't make Mama remind you again."

Robby pushed the food around on his plate, barely eating more than a few mouthfuls.

"Now how are you going to be able to play on Daddy's team if you don't get big and strong and eat your food? Here, take a bite of mashed potatoes. Let's put some meat on those cute little bones."

She prayed that when his lanky frame filled out, his muscles would also develop over time. Sometimes Coop's handsome face would distort like a demon when he fumbled during their afternoon secret playtime. His cheeks flushed crimson, and he swiped the objects to the ground when he couldn't grab them after the second try. Jocelyn attempted to calm her son by stroking his silky hair while she held him in her arms, usually making his tension melt away.

After an episode when Robby's volcanic temper couldn't be calmed, he slammed his head against the kitchen table. As an angry red welt began to erupt on his smooth forehead, Jocelyn knew it was time to tell her husband.

That evening, Rowdy tossed his leather team jacket on the couch when he entered the modest house. Robby darted toward his dad, who scooped him up and tossed him in the air, dangerously close to the whirring blades of the fan hanging from the low ceiling. "What's for supper, darlin'?" he called out to Jocelyn.

"Chicken fried steak. I'm letting it set in the batter for a few minutes. Rowdy, I got to talk to you about Robby. I think somethin's wrong with our little guy. He cries way too much."

"You're always coddling him. You're making a mama's baby out of our son. That's why he's so namby-pamby—always whining. It's time for him to go to preschool and be with other boys. That's what he needs. A little teamwork."

"Today was worse than usual. I swear he's going to hurt himself if we don't do something." Jocelyn shook the excess flour off the cutlets and dropped them into the skillet of spattering oil.

"There's nothing wrong with him that a little whuppin' wouldn't help. Enough said, woman. Let's eat!"

"But he's awfully quiet. Sometimes he gets a dreamy look in his eyes."

Rowdy banged his fist on the table, and Jocelyn's spatula plummeted to the floor. "Well, right now the only thing I'm dreaming about is supper. How 'bout it?"

Over the years as Robby grew up, he remained shy, seldom making himself the center of attention. Jocelyn insisted he enroll in drama class to build his confidence in public speaking. Coach made him work out with weights daily to add bulk while he kept gaining inches in height almost monthly, outgrowing shoes faster than his folks could replace them.

Between managing the equipment at football practices and memorizing his lines for play rehearsals, there was hardly time for any original thinking or emotions of his own. He was steadily developing the blank canvas that makes for a perfect actor.

Robby Preston Cooper got his big break at the historic theater in Austin, Texas. The restored movie palace was the location of a nationwide talent search, with the winner to receive a Hollywood audition for producer Abram Geller's upcoming television show set on a college campus. The casting cattle call sought to fill the part of a Texas boy with a football scholarship for an upcoming show called *Passing Plays*. It was also a publicity stunt cooked up by the network promotions department to build awareness about the television program among high school and college-aged audiences across the country.

While her husband was putting his team through their morning drills, Jocelyn and her seventeen-year-old son made the drive to Austin. They passed rows of rust-colored maize planted in the rich black earth. They finally spotted the dome of the Texas State Capitol. Jocelyn navigated through the traffic in downtown Austin, clutching both hands tightly on the steering wheel.

"Darlin', I'll just do a little shopping while you're at the audition. It'll be a change from my usual trip to the bargain store at home."

"Mama, one day I'm going to be able to buy you anything you want. You'll be treated like a queen, I promise."

"What I want most is for you to be happy doing something that speaks to your soul. Don't worry about Coach. I'll smooth things over with your dad when you win the part."

"*If* I win."

"That doesn't sound like the positive attitude Mr. Elkins has been preaching about for the past three years."

Jocelyn searched for a parking space along Capitol Avenue, but the business district was packed. She double-parked in front of the historic theater and hoped the police wouldn't give her a ticket.

"I'll come get you when you finish. Don't worry about how much time you need. My shopping won't take long, and I'll be back in plenty of time," she said.

"See ya later, Mama." He gave her a quick kiss and flashed an endearing smile.

"Now that's my best guy. It kills me to say it, but break a leg, darlin'."

Two hours later, the afternoon sun turned the dome of the Texas State Capitol into a glowing crown on the building. Jocelyn shielded her eyes from the glare and searched for a parking space near the theater. As she moved slowly past the entrance, Robby raced to her car, wildly waving his arms. She stopped, and he swung open the door and slid in.

"Guess what, Mama. I made the team. We're going to Hollywood!"

6
SIRENA

"FRANCINE, WHERE THE HELL ARE YOU AND COOP?" Charlie shouted into the phone, standing on the red carpet. She strained to catch a glimpse of Coop's vehicle down the crowded boulevard. The line of long black limousines en route to the awards ceremony seemed endless.

"I can see the row of golden Constance statues in front. We're just three cars away, right behind the white stretch," Francine replied.

"Coop's going to have to make an end run for the theater when you get closer," Charlie said.

The pearly white car crawled to the curb. Red carpet interviewer Judy Simmons hovered like a tiger ready to pounce as the oversized car door began to open. She shoved a microphone into Sirena's face as the glittering star emerged from the vehicle like Botticelli's *The Birth of Venus* on a half shell.

"Girl, you took your sweet time getting here. What gives?" Judy asked, smiling without any part of her face in motion, frozen by wrinkle fillers. She batted her thick fringe of false eyelashes as she bent to give Sirena an air kiss.

"We just stopped for a quick bite at Burger-Blast. A girl's got to keep her strength up for the big night ahead," Sirena said. She gingerly placed her adorned sandal onto the red carpet, a modern-day Cinderella emerging from an enchanted coach.

"Oh my gawd, you need an armored truck just for the shoes, let alone that blue sparkling boulder perched between your two gorgeous mountain peaks," Judy gushed.

Sirena stood fully upright with her shoulders back, displaying her physical and gemstone treasures front and center. Judy kept talking nonstop, hardly catching her breath so Sirena could respond. Being interviewed by Judy during the pre-Movie Constellation Awards show was every star's dream. A nominee for Lead Actress, Sirena was in no hurry to end this curbside tête-à-tête with the scrappy queen of the red carpet interviews.

Sirena's date stepped out of the car and headed toward the two women. Judy edged closer to the star's flawless face and asked, "So are you flying solo tonight?"

"No, I've got Ethan Dean Traynor in the cockpit." Sirena giggled and turned to look for her boyfriend. "Here he comes."

"What naughty things were you and Ethan doing in the back of the limo that took you so long to get here? Oh, never mind." Judy mugged for the camera, poking her fingers back and forth, gesturing like a horny frat boy. She turned to Ethan, who had come into the camera shot and put his arms around Sirena.

"So Ethan, when are you going put a ring on her finger and make an honest woman out of her? Not some speck you'd need a microscope to see; I'm talking some major bling."

Sirena paused to collect her thoughts, vowing to herself that Judy wasn't going to make her say something she'd regret on an evening that might be the most memorable night of her life. With a smile that could disarm any foe, she said, "Thanks, Judy. You're a love, but I've got to go. They're asking me to hurry inside." Sirena puckered her plump lips into a smooch aimed at the television viewing audience and then glided down the fabled red carpet into a throng of reporters.

Trailing after her, Judy blurted, "And what's the movie you're up for this year?" She watched Sirena stopping to chat with Judy's competitor from another network. In a close-up, Judy whispered to the camera, "Where would that broad be without Coop?"

Meanwhile, Sirena's limousine, a great white albatross, remained stalled in its spot so no other stars could arrive in style on the red carpet. The event's traffic team in yellow-and-black slickers swarmed the vehicle. Braving the torrents, the frantic transportation manager banged on the hood. He shouted over the crescendo of honking limos, "Man, you've got to get this puppy moving. Show's about to start!"

Max grimaced, feigning concern. "Dang if I know what's up. I can't seem to get this sucker in gear."

Nearby, Charlie covered her face, peering through the latticework of her fingers, as her biggest star sat trapped in his car away from the arrival spot on the red carpet.

Jamaal Kenter from Silverlake studio security had been called to investigate the stalled vehicle—to enforce the strict rule that all cars had to be kept moving away from the entrance. The rain escalated, and unrelenting drops appeared magnified in the glaring headlights of the white stretch limousine.

7

FRANCINE

CHARLIE WHISPERED INTO HER CELL, "Francine, Sirena's aced us at the red carpet! That little bitch has blocked up the arrival area. Her car won't budge, and now she's hogging the press."

"Exactly what *we* tried to do. Look, the only thing I care about right now is Coop, and I suggest you get someone to push that piece of crap out of the way or to blow it up," Francine said, sitting next to her star client who was about to explode with rage in the limo.

"With all this Homeland Security at the theater, careful what you say. Nothing's private on a cell. Stay in the limo line; in about a minute you might have to get Coop to make a run for it. I'll tell Jamaal to prepare to keep everyone away from our boy if he has to get out in the street. Gabe is here at the arrival spot waiting for your car," Charlie said.

"Oh, Coop will *really* go for that plan," Francine said and chewed her fingernail. "But it will get him some extra ink in the press tomorrow. I can see it now: Soaked Star Hangs Lead Actor Competition Out to Dry." She hung up.

"Gabe, move your butt into the driver's seat of that white limo and see if you can work some of your special magic," Charlie said.

"Right. I'm on it like white on rice!" Gabe dashed into the rain and ordered Max to let him take a stab at getting the car started.

Max held his ground, saying no one but he was authorized to drive because of insurance reasons. Gabe ordered the driver to try to start the limo again. Max slid the key in the ignition, pumped the gas, and the massive V-8 engine *miraculously* resurrected, purring like a kitten.

"Guess it's not flooded anymore," Max said sheepishly.

"Move this mother right now! Charlie will investigate this whole thing tomorrow," Gabe said, slamming the door shut. He tried to repress a slight smile, enjoying the heady rush that came from his first taste of authority.

Coop's car slowly claimed the prime arrival spot. Francine turned to him and brushed her lips across his smooth cheek. "You're on, sweetheart. Let's knock 'em dead!"

As Coop extended his long legs out of the limo, Francine exhaled deeply with relief at how another catastrophe had been averted—part of her job as damage control, image protector, and babysitter. She trailed a few steps behind him, just out of the camera angle, almost invisible in her simple black gown. Her cropped brown hair with striking streaks stayed tucked neatly behind her ears, even though chilly gusts whipped the leaky awning. In the fifty-degree temperature, her star necklace felt like a chip of ice against her skin.

Francine had been along for the ride with Coop from the start of his film career. As owner of the reigning Hollywood public relations firm, Darten Publicity International, she was always on the lookout for new clients she could cultivate for both television and film projects. Her firm had a reputation for playing hardball by being overly protective. Francine relished the challenge of representing the newest young television star. If Preston Cooper made it big, she would get her spike-heeled foot on the ground floor of his film career.

In the early 1990s, Francine usually tried to make sure she watched *Passing Plays* on Thursday nights or had one of her assistants tape it to keep track of the progress of Preston Cooper, the hot young lead on the show. She assured herself that jailbait really wasn't her style; she simply couldn't ignore the new kid's charisma and sex appeal, and she knew he was actually over eighteen. She was certain Coop would attract all demographics because he was slightly self-effacing, which was unthreatening to male audiences. He was a looker whose striking face with eyes the color of the Pacific Ocean would appeal to females of all ages. She noted that many of the top Hollywood male stars had arresting blue eyes such as Paul Newman, Robert Redford, and Brad Pitt.

Francine had targeted Preston Cooper for quite a while. She had wanted to land him as a client so she could shepherd his metamorphosis from being a weekly regular in people's living rooms to becoming an icon on the big screen. The buzz around town was that director Jason Hardon was in preproduction for a new teen movie. She had heard that Coop had landed the role in a film version of a vintage sixties situation comedy. He'd play the cool high school stud, once again capitalizing on his good looks.

Hardon was one of the few top directors who hadn't hired Francine as a publicist for his movies. He was being honored at the American Cinema Support annual dinner, and Francine vowed she would ambush him at the event and convince him to hire her as the publicist for the movie. She was accompanying a pair of A-list stars to the ACSG dinner, but there would be plenty of time to work the room.

Francine showed up early at the Rodeo Grande Hotel in Beverly Hills and waited for her clients to arrive on the red carpet. Velvet ropes restrained the gawking crowds, holding them away from the steady stream of celebrity arrivals.

The main ballroom buzzed with movie talk, and participants at the gala milled around the room like a swarm of fireflies. Francine spotted Arthur and Teeni Fielgood heading for a prime table adjacent to the stage. Teeni's course never wavered, but her gregarious husband stopped to bear-hug men and plant sloppy kisses on the lips of most of the female stars he passed.

Teeni shifted her weight from side to side, waiting for her husband to slowly wind his way down a short set of stairs to the main floor until he reached her at the table. "Artie, I'd rather stay home than sit on the second tier behind that awful railing. I guess those little people can say they were here, but they're hardly where the action is. Look, we're closer to the stage than Jason Hardon's table."

"Glad you're happy, Tee. But he's in the middle of the room so the celebs giving testimonials can surround him. It also allows for more varied camera angles for the telecast."

"I'd rather be right next to the stage," Teeni said.

Heading down the aisle, Francine double-checked the number on her place card and searched for her table in the back of the main level. The room vibrated with people drinking, talking, and table-hopping.

The loudspeaker blared, and an usher insistently rang hand chimes to persuade the reluctant crowd gathered around the lobby bar to disperse and take their seats in the ballroom.

Francine had always enjoyed the ACSG event, which seemed more like a great big party instead of the intense rivalry of other awards shows. Many of the attendees had connections with the honoree, and most hoped they'd ingratiate themselves even more by paying homage to Hardon by buying a full table of ten seats.

Francine inched through the maze of tables, working her way to the front. Finally she reached Arthur and tapped him on the shoulder. He stood and gave her a hug that smashed her breasts against him.

Teeni looked up, her eyebrows soaring to even greater heights on her baby-smooth forehead. With her crystal goblet raised aloft, she announced, "This wine is pure swill! If you haven't tried it yet, don't bother."

"Tee, it's a fund-raiser for film restoration, so what'd you expect?" Arthur said, releasing his grip on Francine.

"Better than this stuff," she said, refusing to be upbraided by her husband. "Get me a black napkin before my outfit looks like hell—and some good champagne," she snapped at the waiter. He whisked away her glass.

In a few seconds the waiter reappeared and positioned a sparkling flute of bubbly at her place setting.

At first Francine was miffed at the lowly location of her table in the outskirts of the ballroom, but after hearing Teeni's remark, she soothed herself with the thought that there was often a great price to pay for sitting with the top brass.

The announcer boomed in deep tones like the voice of God, "Ladies and Gentlemen, please take your seats."

At the main table, two chairs facing the stage remained empty like a pair of vacant thrones. From the balcony, a brace of trumpeters announced the arrival of Hollywood royalty. Jason Hardon, looking distinguished in a tuxedo, entered with his entourage in tow. He walked a few steps in front of his wife, Susan. He maneuvered through the tables, barraged with pats on his back as he passed. The crowd stood and applauded when he assumed the place of honor, looking sufficiently embarrassed by the attention.

A host of stars who had appeared in Hardon's films were scattered throughout the glittery room. At the next table, perennial ingénue Suzi Walden was wrapped in a saffron satin gown with a matching oversized bow corralling her golden hair. Francine spotted Mickey Jay Sommers, a former teen megastar. She hoped Coop would land similar iconic parts that she could promote.

The show announcer said in dulcet tones, "Tonight we're here to honor a man of inestimable talent and vision. Ladies and gentlemen, the American Cinema Support Group salutes Jason Hardon as this year's Lifetime Achievement recipient."

Previous award recipients dotted the room, and other film greats were seated at a ring of tables surrounding Hardon.

President of the ACSG Samuel P. Levinson teetered to the microphone. Recovering from a recent stroke, his left lip drooped unceremoniously as he spoke. The veteran movie producer loudly "shushed" into the microphone, emitting a shower of spittle in an attempt to quiet the crowd. He wiped his mouth with a crusty handkerchief and adjusted his thick, black-rimmed glasses. "Some of you took *The Long Way to Happiness* to get here tonight," he said, referring to Hardon's hit film.

The audience quickly found the puns of the honoree's movie titles tedious. A low collective groan wafted across the room, and then conversations began to escalate to a high pitch.

Levinson continued, "We're thrilled that Jason Hardon is here tonight at this ACSG event to be the *Big Man on Campus!*"

Flashing across the big-screen monitors on both sides of the room, the camera cut to a wide-eyed Mickey Jay giving his signature two-fingered salute he made famous in the hit teen film about a short guy trying to make the basketball squad. The audience noise rose to a deafening din, and a constant trickle of people escaped from their tables and headed for the lobby bar.

"He's been a writer, producer, and director. Jason Hardon has woven laughter and warmth into the fabric of the American cinema. We are here to honor him tonight. Let's show this movie great our appreciation."

The nine other people at Hardon's table, starting with his wife, rose to their feet, and slowly the whole audience stood and applauded like a wave in a football stadium. The unseen announcer blared over the loudspeakers, "We'll be right back with Pricilla the Poodle from *Priceless Pooch* right after a word from our sponsors."

Francine headed for the main table, stopping along the way to schmooze with stars who were her clients or with studio executives who paid the bills for her services. She waited patiently behind Jason Hardon until he was released from a clench from Arthur Fielgood. She stepped back to keep an arm's length from Arthur.

"Frannie, come up to my office and see me sometime," Arthur said as he headed back to Teeni.

"Jason, congratulations on tonight!" Francine said. "Wonderful to see comedy receive the recognition it deserves."

"Thanks, Francine. How's the world been treating you these days?"

"Super, but I'm really interested in what's shaking with you. That sixties sitcom remake's got my interest. Has the studio signed on a publicist yet? I could do some big things with Preston Cooper if given the chance. I think he's got the whole package."

"Give my people a call and I'll take a meeting. Good to see you, Francine."

"Ten seconds, everyone," the announcer blared. The crowd instantly settled in their seats.

Presenter Suzi Walden stood at the microphone, trying to remain calm as the latest generation of Pricilla the Poodle left a knee-level trail of drool on her satin gown. "Tonight we're here to honor Jason Hardon, who wrote *Priceless Pooch,* among many other comedy classics."

On cue from her trainer in the wings, Pricilla's perky bark signaled the animal's enthusiasm. Suzi gave the dog a pat on the head and then blew a sweeping kiss to her former director.

"Now let's welcome America's hottest new actor from the television show *Passing Plays,* Preston Cooper, soon to star in Jason Hardon's upcoming film," the announcer said.

Coop loped to the stage, displaying his dazzling smile and killer physique. He stooped to speak into the microphone that was set for pint-sized Suzi. "Mr. Hardon, it's a dream come true to be in one of your movies. I've been a fan of yours ever since I was young."

The remark drew approving laughter from the crowd since Coop was still under twenty.

My mission is accomplished, Francine thought.

Tomorrow she would try to get assigned as the publicist on Hardon's film at Silverlake Pictures and secure her chance to work with Preston Cooper. She could feel in her bones that he was the real deal—with potentially huge box office and sex appeal.

8
CHARLIE & ARTHUR

Publicist Francine Darten and Charlie Wallach at Silverlake Pictures had forged a working relationship over the years that had all the stability of a teeter-totter. They appeared to be warm and fuzzy while a picture was in the works, but the climate cooled when there was a hiatus.

Charlie called Gabe into her office to give him some advice she had been told when she first started in the movie business.

"Hey, what's up?" Gabe adjusted his glasses and focused on Charlie.

"Take a listen. You've been privy to a lot of back-and-forth lately between Francine and me. I want to set you straight. You came from marketing package goods and know a lot about personal care products, but the film industry is different. Heaven knows, I've used my share of deodorant from working up a sweat in this business!"

"I also worked on feminine sprays. Thank goodness I moved on before all hell broke loose with lawsuits against our products."

"Now they've got a spray for every nook and cranny of the body. But enough about keeping everything high and dry! You've been at Silverlake Pictures for a while, but I want to pass along something I was told early on when I started working at a movie studio."

Gabe sat on the sofa and stroked his stubbled chin.

Charlie pulled a chair near him. "Years ago I received a bouquet from a big star after the weekend of the box office smash that I handled. I was so jazzed that he even knew who I was, much less sent me a present. But a few months later when we wanted him to appear at a charity baseball game, his assistant wouldn't return my calls or emails. It was like he had disappeared from the face of the earth."

Didn't his contract make him participate?" Gabe asked.

"No, he was already involved with his next film project. My supervisor at the studio told me that 'if they call you, it's not personal; and if they don't call you, it's not personal.'"

"You mean you can't have real relationships in the movie business?"

"Not exactly, Gabe. In Hollywood, business friendships sometimes last as long as the film is at stake."

"So everyone uses everyone else to get ahead, I guess." The wheels in Gabe's head seemed to be turning as the space between his brows knotted.

"You can make some real friends along the way, and they should be cherished. I try to break through and not automatically assume the worst. There are exceptions, thank goodness." Charlie said. "Hey, don't look so glum."

Gabe mustered a roguish smile.

Charlie leaned forward. "The movie studio puts up the money to develop, produce, and market a motion picture. But the director, the production company, and even the talent think they're in charge. The big stars call the shots about what they will or won't do to promote a picture even if it affects the cash in their pockets.

"Due to back-end deals, right?" Gabe added.

Charlie nodded in agreement. "Take a powerhouse like Steven Spielberg. He's like that eight-hundred-pound gorilla who can sit wherever he wants—because he *always* delivers the goods!"

"I've always heard it's a major bullshit detector if someone refers to him as Steve instead of Steven," Gabe said, hoping to sound like an insider instead of a complete novice.

"Yeah, there's always some braggart who boasts loudly enough for any nearby starlets to hear how he just left a development meeting with Stevie Spielberg."

Charlie patted Gabe on the shoulder. "Cheer up. You just watch; it's always fun to see fledgling directors try to throw their weight around when they haven't got an ounce of leverage. If through the studio's advice their films have improved and do some decent box office revenues, they think they're king or queen of the world."

In contrast, Charlie had found it a pleasure to work with action star Kramer Knight. He was a dynamo who treated everyone with respect.

Arthur had called a meeting with the hulking actor to discuss plans for him to appear as Guest Mayor of Hollywood for a movie promotion. Most big-name celebrities would turn up their noses at such common duty—shaking hands and kissing babies, shamelessly hawking their latest film—but Kramer was willing to support a motion picture if it would help fill theaters and add revenue to his back-end deal. Kramer Knight was a marketing department's poster boy.

Some top stars were great to work with, and others were challenges, like Sirena Jackson. She seemed to enjoy her reputation of being a demanding diva.

Usually the staff at Silverlake Pictures kept their cool when major talent strolled through the offices in the twenty-story, silver-reflective glass building. Insiders generally frowned upon showing signs of being starstruck, although some earned the distinction of being "star-fuckers," sycophants who pandered to the wants and needs of celebrities or were merely content to bask in their limelight.

As a vice president, Charlie maintained a businesslike demeanor at most times, but she tried to find an avenue to make personal connections. A starlet might divulge to her about a producer who had tried to get a blow job for the promise of a part. Charlie occasionally had the ear of the big brass, depending on which alliances were being formed at the time.

In Charlie's streamlined contemporary office, one of her most treasured pieces of movie memorabilia was displayed on her desk: a vintage photo of silent film diva Lois Larue. She was Charlie's favorite actress and the muse to many early Hollywood directors.

In an off-the-cuff remark at a meeting, film director Lawrence Larue had boasted about his relationship with the film star. "Lois Larue is my great aunt. You can meet her anytime you want. Just say the word."

Charlie took the bait and said, "Let's see you deliver the goods."

On the following Monday morning when everyone was focused on dissecting the weekend grosses, Gabe flew into Charlie's office. "You won't believe who's in the lobby."

"Way too early for guessing games. I give up. Who?" Charlie asked wearily.

"Lois Larue. She's with Lawrence Larue. I thought she was dead!"

"Don't tell her that! What the hell are we doing standing here?" Charlie smoothed her skirt and headed to greet Miss Larue.

Chatting with the receptionist, the outline of the "Everything Girl" was reduced to an ethereal sprite at barely five feet tall. Gabe lunged forward to hold the door open for his boss, and Charlie smiled broadly at the living legend in the lobby. The screen siren's murky eyes sparkled, lighting up her face that still retained a glimmer of her former beauty.

"Charlie Wallach, may I present Miss Lois Larue. Charlie's a vice president here," Lawrence said.

"It's a great pleasure to meet you. Let's not stand out here in the lobby." Charlie turned to the receptionist. "Tell Arthur we have a very special visitor."

Lawrence clutched his great aunt's elbow as she glided down the hall in a flowing tea-length gown as pale as her ivory skin. In a parade, Lawrence, Charlie, Gabe, and the "Everything Girl" made their way down the marble corridor toward Arthur's corner office. Out of every doorway and cubicle along the way, secretaries abandoned their desks, and their supervisors jumped in front of them to get a better view, spilling into the hallways. Soon the department came to a grinding halt. The staff's blasé attitudes toward celebrity melted as Miss Larue made a special appearance with an appeal far greater than any modern movie star.

Gabe detoured and returned to his desk. Arthur Fielgood emerged at the door of his office. He shook Miss Larue's delicate hand and, for once, didn't try to kiss a star on the lips. He ushered the visitors into a pair of boxy leather-and-chrome chairs in his cavernous office. The ancient movie star looked like a china doll nestled into the sculptural seat, with her legs dangling.

As Charlie entered the room, Arthur said, "Miss Larue, have you met my girl Friday?"

"I guess you're not talking about my old chum, that glorious broad Rosalind Russell who starred with Cary Grant in *His Girl Friday*. But yes, I've had the distinct pleasure of meeting Miss Wallach when I arrived, Mr. Fielgood."

"Call me Arthur," he said and sat behind his massive desk.

"I've always thought working for the studios was a bitch! In my day, I was chained to a shitty contract." Lois spoke slowly with a high-pitched

Bronx accent, the main factor for her failure to transition to talkies when sound became the rage in films in the late 1920s. "Miss Wallach, darling, get that photograph of me that my nephew mentioned you have in your office. I used to have to pose lying on a couch or a bed for hours with my hair hanging down seductively, which actually gave me a humdinger of a headache."

Charlie dashed down the hall to retrieve the dramatic portrait. When she returned, Lawrence pulled out his cell phone camera and started capturing his great aunt autographing the vintage print that had been liberated from its frame.

Arthur mashed the button on his phone and instructed his secretary in rapid-fire, "Amy, call the studio photographer and get him over here on the double!"

Arthur wanted to preserve the photo op for himself. It wasn't every day a true film pioneer was sitting in his office. Movie stars came and went, but Lois Larue was eternal.

Gabe's head popped through the half-open door of Arthur's office. "Charlie, Francine Darten says it's an emergency—code red. She's got to talk to you *pronto*."

"Sorry, guys, but we've got a picture to release. It's been great to meet you, Miss Larue. You've always been one of my heroes. I'll call you later, Lawrence. You're truly a man of your word," Charlie said.

Lois slowly extricated herself from the chair and wrapped her reedlike arms around Charlie's waist. "Sister, you've got plenty of moxie, and make sure you use it where it counts!"

Charlie kissed her heavily rouged cheek and then dashed out of the office.

Warily eyeing Arthur, the Hollywood icon said, "What goes around comes around, bubba."

M OST OF THE TIME, CHARLIE wished she could pummel Arthur Fielgood. He had inherited her on his staff when he assumed the post as the head of the department.

At his former job, his second-in-command moved to snatch the top spot as president at another studio, so Arthur was bereft of his usual right-hand man when he started at Silverlake Pictures. It was always rumored that Arthur grabbed all the credit for his coworker's ideas and marketing coups.

Since Charlie had two years to go on her contract, Arthur decided to give her a try before possibly handing her a pink slip, which was actually a pair of golden handcuffs. If he fired her, he would be effectively giving her a two-year paid vacation.

Arthur Fielgood enjoyed keeping his marketing team at odds with each other, never letting his staff feel completely secure in their positions. On rare occasions when it was advantageous for him, he singled out Charlie Wallach for special recognition. Although she made a six-figure salary, had a generous car allowance, a decent parking spot, and an expense account, he insisted on referring to Charlie as "his girl Friday," or "the marketing gal." She had pointed out to him on numerous occasions that she preferred to be referred to by her correct title of vice president. Arthur reformed for a short period but would invariably revert to his old habits.

As President of Marketing, Arthur took pride in being the only generalist in the department. He supervised his team that handled research, media, publicity, promotions, and events.

Charlie had climbed the ladder at the studio from a humble start. With a good word from her roommate Cindy who was dating Sean Shannigan, head of the art department at Silverlake Pictures, Charlie got her first break in the movie industry—a field where *who* you know can often count more than *what* you know. Cindy eventually became the third new-and-improved Mrs. Sean Shannigan.

When Charlie started at Silverlake, she found out that working at a major movie studio wasn't all the glitz and glamour of premieres and junkets; it was a twenty-four seven commitment, especially at the bottom rung of the ladder. She set her sights on shattering the glass ceiling and climbing her way to the executive floor.

Charlie had studied entertainment marketing in college and was thankful she had completed a film history course that introduced her to silent films legends, including Lois Larue, Buster Keaton, and Charlie Chaplin. She learned how the motion picture industry evolved with many of the early movie companies locating in the Silver Lake area of Los Angeles. While the director of the Keystone comedies Mack Sennett's studio did not survive the Great Depression and cowboy star Tom Mix's venture failed, a handful of studios flourished to become giants, including her current employer, Silverlake Pictures.

The studio star system, in which the talent was groomed and handled under strict contracts, crumbled when the actors eventually took control of their careers and paychecks in the 1960s. Charlie knew her job was much different than the old days of Hollywood when the stars had to comply with the studios' demands.

At her first job in the real world outside of college, Charlie read the daily entertainment trades, kept her eyes and ears open in the workplace, and hoped she could learn quickly enough to progress. She eagerly picked up the intricacies and value of product tie-ins during the advertising phase of the launch of a motion picture. She steadily moved up the corporate ladder.

The powwows to discuss upcoming promotional and media campaigns were held in a conference room known as "Camelot." It had been the brainstorm of one administrative regime to name the common spaces in the office tower at Silverlake Pictures with clever titles. Instead of referring to conference room one, two, or three, they were called "Larry," "Curly," and "Moe." The mailroom was "Shemp," the fourth, lesser-known Stooge.

In Camelot, a massive ornately carved round table dominated the room, fabricated as a prop for the return-of-the-swashbuckler film, *Lancelot in Love*. The cabinets that housed the high-tech equipment had been carefully hand-hewn to duplicate the details on the oak Arthurian table. Swiveling executive desk chairs upholstered in tapestries depicting jousting knights added an anachronistic touch. This Camelot was the scene of many fierce business battles, but no one seemed to have minded that its musical namesake from the sixties was a release from a rival studio, MGM.

Leather-bound marketing plans with the film title embossed in gold for one of the summer releases, *BH Princess for a Day*, were placed in front of each chair. Sirena Jackson played a starving actress who won her wish-come-true on a game show. It wasn't a fresh Cinderella story, but the studio often tried to minimize its downside risk by producing remakes or familiar themes.

To plan the advertising campaign, President of Marketing Arthur Fielgood, Executive Producer Paten Jeffries, President of Production

Carl Atkins, and other members of the marketing team filled the chairs in the Camelot conference room.

Arthur Fielgood designated himself as the head of the round table without ends by keeping the seats adjacent to him vacant. The space between him and the rest of the participants gave him room to flail his arms if he needed to make a point. He started the meeting. "Charlie, why don't you set the scene for our campaign?"

Startled at being asked to participate when she had been ignored for the previous three sessions, Charlie took a deep breath. Arthur's aftershave with strong overtones of musk swirled into her nostrils, and she willed herself not to sneeze. She searched her memory for the pivotal scene she had read in the script several months before. The primary shooting had just begun, and she hadn't gone to the studio screening room to see the dailies.

Charlie stood by her chair and began her presentation. "Sirena, as Sammie Smyth, counts the change in her purse to pay her water bill after standing in a long line."

"Yes, that's the action before the expositional scene where she's telling her best friend she wishes she were as rich as the Kardashians," producer Paten Jeffries added.

Charlie continued, "Her roommate was supposed to go on the game show, *BH Princess for a Day*, but she got sick. Sammie takes her place and crushes the opponents. She starts her spending spree on the posh part of Rodeo Drive, but she craves a taco from a food truck instead of eating a fancy meal at a chic spot for 'ladies-who-lunch.'"

Arthur raised his hand to stop the progression of her tale. "Sean, show Paten the layouts for the one-sheets you've come up with."

Sean Shannigan, the head of Silverlake's art department, lined up five versions of movie posters along the wooden railing, with the graphics turned toward the wall. He had been instructed to create a joke tag line to start the presentation.

Arthur turned the first poster with a flourish. A full-color, heavily retouched photograph showed Sirena Jackson in a skin-tight dress, downing a slice of pizza and licking a hint of tomato sauce from her lips. He read the gag headline, "What a Spicy, Hot Piece!"

Everyone laughed heartily except Charlie.

"Sirena looks superhot in that dress. We got the designer to lower the neckline, which really showcases her curves," Sean said.

The rest of the posters featured the proposed headline, "She's a Real Royal Pain."

Charlie flipped to the product promotions page in the marketing plan. "Paten, we've landed a great tie-in with Pizza Pan Party. They'll put up twenty million in advertising."

Arthur beamed with pride at the clever one-sheet design and the arrangement that would save the studio millions of dollars in advertising. "Media will schedule Pizza Pan Party spots for a four-week television flight."

Paten leaped to his feet like a man in a hot seat. "What the fuck do you think *that* is?"

"What the hell are you talking about?" Arthur retorted, his face turning from his perennial golden tan to crimson.

"That fucking slice of pizza is what I'm talking about! We've already shot the scene with Sirena eating a taco. You can't run a campaign with a slice of pizza in her fist. I'm the producer, for Chrissake!"

"The hell I can't," Arthur bellowed. "The people in my department have worked their fannies off to get this deal. You just don't tell Pizza Pan Party to take a hike, especially when they ponied up the big bucks for the campaign. The new Pictland Films animated flick is nipping at our heels, and they'll get those Pizza Pan Party promotional dollars if we don't sign on the dotted line here and now!"

Sean started to gather the mock-ups of the posters he had designed. It wasn't the first time he had seen his layouts shot down in a matter of seconds. "Guess it's back to the proverbial drawing board, right, Arthur?"

"Don't touch a goddamn thing," Arthur barked, his eyes narrowed to slits. "Carl, we need to reshoot the taco scene!"

"Arthur, did you forget who's in charge of production? Marketing doesn't make the movies, remember? I do!" Carl said.

"Yeah, I remember I've got to sell whatever shoots out the pipeline."

"Nice shot, Arthur. I'll remember those words. For your information, the movie has been in production for three weeks. With a change like this, we'll run over budget and get behind schedule." Carl picked up a layout featuring the pizza and tossed it across the table. "We've already knocked the set."

"Paten, just because you're the producer, you might think it's your movie, but our money made it. I say we need to reshoot! Carl, your job as the head of Production is to do it. I'm not giving up this pizza promotion!" Arthur slammed his palm on the wooden table.

"Let's just run our little difference of opinion by Manny. After all, he *is* the Chairman of the Motion Picture Group," Carl said.

"Run it by Jesus H. Christ, for all I care! I'll phone him myself right now," Arthur said, hitting his intercom. "Amy, get me Manny Silverstein, on the double!"

Carl clutched a magic marker and slashed a murderous red *X* across the slice of pizza. "You arrogant asshole!"

Arthur glared at his nemesis across the table. In calmer tones on the phone, he said, "Manny, it's Arthur. We've gotta reshoot a scene on *BH Princess for a Day*. Otherwise a twenty-million-dollar co-op with Pizza Pan Party is going down faster than a cheerleader after the prom. Tell Carl to get those cameras rolling!" He punched the speakerphone button so the group could hear the response.

Manny's raspy voice boomed, "Carl, just make it happen! Pizza had better be just as goddamned sexy as tacos. I'm not leaving millions on the table!" He ended the call.

Carl hurled the marker in Arthur's direction and stormed out of the meeting. A hushed silence fell over the conference room.

A broad smile spread like a rainbow across Arthur's stormy face as he clapped his hands together in triumph. "That's the magic of moviemaking! Charlie, make sure those Pizza Pan Party contracts are signed and in my office by nine tomorrow morning." He swiveled in his chair and said, "Why the hell are all of you hanging around Camelot? I'm suddenly hungry for a slice of pizza. Meeting's adjourned!"

10

BIG HOUSE,
LITTLE LADY

EVENTUALLY CHARLIE MADE HER DISTINGUISHING mark at Silverlake Pictures in marketing. The department was responsible for implementing wacky publicity stunts to bring attention to the latest releases and also to stage the budget-bulging premieres. Usually the elaborate parties were held to get network and print coverage of the movies, and A-list stars were invited to add glamour to the events.

Although Charlie was in charge of working with companies who would partner with the studio to promote their brands, at times the whole marketing team was asked for input on big picture ideas. In a brainstorming session, Charlie mustered all her creativity to come up with a concept for the premiere of *Big House, Little Lady* that would amaze even the most jaded Hollywood partygoers. The film was Silverlake's top shot at Best Picture, and the launch of the movie was crucial to garner media attention.

The updated novel from a century ago featured the box office giant Preston "Coop" Cooper and his wife at the time, Sirena Jackson. The studio wanted to sweep the awards across the board.

Charlie thumbed through a stack of tabloids with Sirena's picture gracing the cover. "Ever since the split, Sirena has emerged as everyone's darling, so she's a shoe-in for the sympathy vote for Lead Actress, augmented by a truly stellar portrayal."

"First the Silver Orbs and then the Movie Constellation Awards." Arthur thought about his quarter-of-a-million-dollar bonus that might come as a reward.

"I've heard some talk that *Big House* might get some special recognition at the Cannes Film Festival," Gabe said, working his way into the conversation.

"You pronounce the festival *can*, not *con*. If you're going to be in the biz, you need to sound like it," Arthur said, wagging his finger at Gabe.

"We've got to make sure that the Silver Orbs voters can get up close and personal with Coop and Sirena. We'll arrange separate press conferences for them," Charlie said.

Gabe jotted down notes while she spoke. He doodled a tin can in the margin.

Arthur grabbed a shiny apple from the crystal bowl of fruit on his desk and rotated it in his palm. "Too bad the good old days of over-the-top cocktail parties and swag bags are forbidden." He crunched a bite of the fruit without offering any to the others. "We used to show the Silver Orbs members a little razzle-dazzle. We've got to think of something fresh to capture their attention."

"How about a private screening of the movie on the studio lot with a champagne reception? Shouldn't that be enough for an awesome film?" Gabe asked.

"We're talking big picture here. We need some heat! Everybody, think!" Arthur commanded.

Gabe sank lower in his seat, hoping Arthur wouldn't hold a grudge against him for offering a tepid suggestion.

The studio felt confident they would reel in a slew of Movie Constellation Awards for *Big House, Little Lady*. Based loosely on

Jack London's obscure novel, *The Little Lady of the Big House*, the story was revised to meet modern sensibilities that required more raw sexuality instead of the unconsummated love from the original book that was published in 1916. The plot had been considered scandalous at the time of its release, but it seemed tame by modern sensibilities.

The screenwriter scrubbed the antiquated text of many of the politically incorrect references about Chinese servants. Most of the poetic dialogue and impromptu songs were excised, and the sex scenes were beefed up enough to get an RR rating.

A love triangle developed between millionaire rancher and farmer Dick Forrest; his vivacious, sensuous wife, Paula; and Evan Graham, an old friend of Dick's who became his houseguest and rival at the centerpiece of the sprawling spread, the Big House.

Sirena was perfectly cast as Paula Forrest, an athletic, wild, sexually aware woman. Her beauty matched London's description of Paula's physical traits with a body that made men stop and take notice. Amelia had been instructed to dye Sirena's platinum hair to a honey-golden hue to portray the horsewoman who could ride like a man and play piano with the verve of a virtuoso instead of the timid parlor skills of the women of the day.

Coop was a natural to portray the irresistible Graham, a hunky interloper. Physically, he fit the character in the novel whose hair was bleached golden from the sun. His cheeks were high-boned, and his mouth was generously proportioned with a strong chin.

Jack London described Graham as "all light and delight, with a hint—but the slightest of hints—of Prince Charming."

Coop knew he could easily play a fantasy lover, but he was determined to give some weight to the moral dilemma of the love triangle. Graham had strength and was described in the book as "strong, simple; been everywhere, seen everything, knows most of a lot of things, straight, square, looks you in the eye—well, in short, a man's man."

Silverlake Pictures set their sights on landing Sirena in the Lead Actress Constance Award race. Although the Dick Forrest character had almost equal screen time to that of Evan Graham, the studio positioned Coop to be considered for the Lead Actor award for his role as the intruder into a seemingly perfect marriage. Ads would run in industry trade journals to lobby Movie Constellation Awards members to vote for the world's biggest box office star as their choice for the top acting prize.

The marketing team at Silverlake Pictures calculated that Brent Wilder, as husband Dick Forrest, would have a better shot at Best Supporting Actor in such a substantial part, eclipsing all contenders with truly secondary roles.

Dick Forrest was described as using innovative farming and ranching techniques. He sowed his wild oats before settling down to build his empire. He met and married Paula and never suffered from jealousy over the effect she had on men. Physically, Dick Forrest was almost a double for his rival, Evan Graham.

The theme of the movie premiere would capitalize on the rural location of the period film set in the fertile Sacramento Valley in the early twentieth century. For the party, barnyards would be erected on the studio backlot with beautiful women in scanty outfits and rugged cowboys on horseback. A replica of the Big House at the event would have food stations in every room with organic farm-to-table fare that would be a nod to the progressive farming techniques that were portrayed in the plot.

In the film, Sirena was toned as tight as a leather drum. She was draped in a diaphanous white bathing suit that clung to her body, exposing her world-famous breasts through the veil of fabric, moving freely while she careened on a black stallion into the swimming hole. She flung her head back in ecstasy as she swayed to the cadence of her steed, gripping its flanks with her knees. When visitor Graham caught sight of the fearless female rider in the water, he was entranced by her laughter and the freedom of her body on view without corsets and stays of the era.

Over and over, he replayed the sensual image in his mind, remembering every curve and her smiling eyes that locked with his—the stranger on horseback next to her husband of a dozen years.

Although Graham and Paula only kiss in the novel, they had scorching sex scenes in the movie, as they were struck with passion on first sight. In furtive trysts, they coupled in the woods and in Paula's exquisite private chambers in the rambling house. Sirena straddled her sex partner in a close-up with full frontal nudity for three seconds, quicker than a wardrobe malfunction on a Sunday football championship game.

Coop had worked out for a month to tighten his glutes for his brief backside shot when he bedded Sirena toward the beginning of the picture. Coop and Sirena almost immolated the screen with their sucking and humping with gleaming body parts that moved in a frantic rhythm that hardly seemed could be interrupted by a director calling for the scene to cut.

The studio was sure the picture would get slapped with an X from the Film Industry Protection Service of America ratings board, FIPSA. Silverlake President of Exhibition Richard Riggins had begged the director to shoot for an RR, the level below a restrictive X.

He explained how to get the preferred RR designation. "Two *fucks* are allowed if it's 'Fuck you!' One *fuck* is okay if it's 'I really want to fuck you.'" He wiped the bead of sweat from his upper lip. "You've got all the above, plus people going every which way but up. I stopped counting f-bombs after a while."

Jack Wesson, the director, argued, "At FIPSA, violence is in the eye of the beholder and nudity gets rated depending on how much flesh shows and who is doing what to whom. I want total creative control."

"If we don't cooperate and self-regulate with FIPSA, the government's going to step in and handle the rating system. Then the shit's really going to hit the fan," Richard said.

"Then we'll just have to duck. The film stands as is!" Jack clinched his teeth.

The marketing team was always negotiating with the ratings board when they were producing their advertising materials. Trailers with sexually explicit content could only be shown with adult-rated movies, and those with family-oriented themes were appropriate for general audiences. The studios searched for ways to gain points on the tracking studies that measured the public's awareness and interest to see films.

Arthur gathered his staff in Camelot and posed the question, "What if you throw an orgy and no one *comes*?"

"Care to be a bit more specific?" Charlie asked, ignoring his double entendre.

"Love scenes with real-life husbands and wives are about as sexy as a cold shower," Arthur said. "We need something that could turn into one of those Hollywood myths: like that star doing it with a rodent. People are still talking about it."

"I don't know about that one," Gabe said.

Charlie shuffled her papers, preparing to discuss the plans for *Big House, Little Lady*. She felt uncomfortable with the gossip-based strategy for marketing the film.

"Let's create some spin that Coop and Sirena were really doing the big nasty," Arthur posed with a sly smile.

"That should add some steam," Gabe said, smiling with satisfaction.

"Now that's what I call goddamned spin!" Arthur said.

11
SIRENA &
AMELIA

"**M**ONTHS BEFORE THE SUPERSTAR COUPLE began filming *Big House, Little Lady*, Sirena said, "Coop, I'm getting tired of being fodder for the tabloids. How many times have they claimed we're living in separate houses?"

"I wish we had a couple more houses, the way prices are going through the roof these days. In fact, I think we should get a beach house in the Malibu Colony when we need a break from Bel Air. We'd better find a good agent to do the legwork because the minute the owner finds out we're looking, the price will jump through the roof," Coop said.

"I guess I can't complain, because my picture is always plastered everywhere," Sirena said.

"Too bad it's never to our advantage. It takes everything I can muster not to deck some of those guys. I wish we could be out and around like everyone else, but we cause a riot wherever we go. It gets old being hounded by the 'paps.'"

"You'll start worrying if people stop caring about what we're doing!" Sirena said.

Coop and Sirena were perpetually besieged by paparazzi. Tabloid publishers had a continuous field day during the couple's romance, marriage, and acrimonious break-up. There was constant speculation about why they didn't have children and who were their lovers. Together or apart, they sold loads of papers.

After meeting on the set of *Best Boy* eight years before, the pair was inseparable. Georgia-born Sirena gushed on a string of interview shows that she had met her soul mate with small-town values like hers. Her bit part in Coop's film launched her career. It wasn't long before their on-screen kisses moved to the bedroom.

Sirena was a down-home girl who became a Hollywood legend by a twist of fate. Like the myth about "the sweater girl" Lana Turner, who was spotted sipping an ice cream soda at the counter of Schwab's Pharmacy on Sunset Boulevard, Sirena Jackson was discovered eating a hot fudge sundae in Hollywood.

The summer after their college freshman year, Sirena and her best friend from high school in Georgia, Amelia Patterson, flew to Los Angeles to spend a week with Amelia's famous uncle Abram Geller and his glamorous young wife, Nicole. Amelia had decided to quit the university and go to cosmetology school instead. Her parents hoped her successful uncle would be able to talk their wayward daughter into staying in college.

The girls borrowed Abram's prized vintage '65 Mustang from his collection of automobiles and went exploring.

They tore out of the ten-car garage from the Bel Air mansion and headed down to Sunset Boulevard through the gates of the affluent section of town. Amelia swerved into a side street to stop at a stand manned by a vendor sitting under an umbrella attached to a sign for Hollywood maps and guidebooks. Sirena jumped out of the passenger seat and bought a guide to the heart of Tinseltown. After a quick glance at the suggested itineraries, they decided to take in the sights along Hollywood Boulevard. They circled their prospective tourist attractions and planned to go first to C.C. Brown's for a treat.

Amelia swore she'd diet *after* she got home from vacation. Sirena's taut midriff peaked out from her cropped T-shirt silk screened with "Georgia Peaches are the Sweetest" stretched tightly across her full, high breasts. The slim typeface on Amelia's T-shirt wasn't quite as extended over her chest. The girls couldn't wait to actually stand on the corner of Hollywood and Vine, picturing it covered in stardust and movie magic.

"Let's go for dessert. I'm in the mood for ice cream," Amelia said.

"You're always in the mood for something sweet. That's why you're with me!" Sirena said,

"Very funny. Let's find C.C. Brown's. It's on the map we bought." She pulled into a parking lot and was handed a ticket by the attendant. "Seven dollars in advance? You've got to be really rich to live in this town," Amelia said, slowly pulling each dollar from her wallet.

The attendant stroked the candy-apple-red paint on the hood of the Mustang and then vaulted into the driver's seat. He screeched around the corner of the lot, parking the car next to a van emblazed with metal ornaments from the tire wells to the rooftop. Brass duckies, sunbursts, along with every imaginable shape, were adhered to the vehicle—a collage on wheels. Sirena hoped she wouldn't find imprints of those little figurines embedded into the door of Amelia's uncle's classic car.

Amelia and Sirena sauntered down the boulevard, giggling at shop windows full of black studded jackets, outlandish wigs, sex toys, and countless movie souvenirs. They were wide-eyed tourists looking for glitz and excitement.

The beep beep of a hand-pumped horn signaled for them to jump aside to make way for a hulking man with a crew cut wearing a hot pink pantsuit, pulled by a pair of matching huskies on rhinestone leashes.

"That's not exactly the kind of glamour I expected in Hollywood!" Sirena said.

"The leashes were cool, but the hair was all wrong." Amelia shook her head in laughter.

The starry-eyed pair stopped at an old-fashioned ice cream parlor, C.C. Brown's, an oasis amid the head shops and tacky stores. A brass bell jingled as they entered the quaint shop. The aroma of chocolate and caramel sauce cooking in the copper kettles masked the traffic fumes and human stench from the street.

They sat at a table for two. "What are you going to have?" Amelia asked.

"The specialty of the house: a hot fudge sundae loaded with mounds of homemade whipped cream."

Amelia grabbed the guidebook and said, "Listen to this: 'In 1906 Clarence Clifton Brown invented the hot fudge sundae. He relocated to Hollywood Boulevard in 1929 and became a favorite of stars like Clark Gable and Mary Pickford.' Do you think Clark Gable actually sat in this seat?"

"Frankly, my friend, I don't have a clue," Sirena said in a deep, smoky drawl.

"Who the hell is Mary Pickford?" Amelia asked.

"A very famous and very rich siren of the American silent screen," an impish man said with a clipped English accent. He held up his hands in front of his face, fashioning a television frame out of the space between his fingers. Catching Sirena in his sights, he turned to the lithe woman in black standing next to him. "She's pe-e-e-r-fect, don't you think, lovey?"

"Um-m-m, Peter, that silvery-blond hair's not the usual Valley-girl dye-job. She could be the one."

Sirena and Amelia looked at each other with crooked smiles that burst into a torrent of schoolgirl giggles. They were getting used to strange people doing strange things in Hollywood.

"The one for what?" Sirena asked. She turned her head abruptly, her platinum hair flipping over her shoulder.

"To appear in an advertisement," the woman said. "Hi, I'm Gretchen Blanchette. I'm doing casting for a New York advertising agency. We're looking for a 'California girl' to feature in a print ad for an affordable automobile. Interested?"

Sirena remembered how her father and stepmother had warned her about con men in Los Angeles. They didn't say anything about con women or con couples.

"Looking for two girls?" Amelia asked. She sat up a little straighter and flipped her hair like Sirena had done.

"Just one pretty blonde," the man answered, prancing around the shop, searching for the best angle in his makeshift finger viewfinder.

"I could be a blonde in about an hour. I'm a hairstylist." Amelia ran her hands through her shoulder-length auburn hair.

"Peter, we've got to move on if she's not interested." Gretchen inched toward the door, clutching her designer satchel.

"I didn't say that I'm not interested. I just can't say yes right now. What's your name and how can I get hold of y'all?" Sirena asked in a deep drawl.

"Sorry, lovey. I'm Peter Churchill. I'm staying at a hotel in Beverly Hills. We're shooting the day after tomorrow. We've got professional models for the rich older couple in the layout, but the client wanted to save a few quid on talent on the young struggling twosome by hiring nonprofessionals. I've already signed up a bloke to be your mate. Drop by my casita at the hotel in about an hour, and we'll take a few test shots and sign the contracts."

"Mate? Am I supposed to be married?" Sirena asked.

"No, *mate* as in *pal*, as you Yanks say. Shall we expect you?"

"We're from Georgia, and we're not Yankees!" Amelia said.

Sirena shot her a look and then smiled angelically at Peter. "Thank you, but I've got to think about it. We're going to hang out around here for a while in Hollywood."

In her heart, she knew it wasn't safe to go with them to the hotel, even though a woman accompanied the man. Sirena didn't want her career or life to end, but Peter and his offer piqued her curiosity.

Amelia whispered to Sirena, "We can call my uncle and check them out. Tell them we'll be there in a couple of hours."

Sirena turned to show Peter her curvy profile. "Okay, it sounds good. We can't get over to Beverly Hills until about five o'clock. Is that too late?"

"Here's my card. We'll see you then, girls," Gretchen said. She scratched the phone number of the hotel on the back. "Sirena, if you want to be a model, I wouldn't eat that sundae." She and Peter walked out into the hazy sunshine, closing the door behind them, followed by the tinkle of the little bell.

"Oh my God, I'm going to be famous!" Sirena shouted. "I always knew I would be. I might start off as a model, but I'm going to be an actress—a movie star!"

"Get a grip, Sirena! We might be from Georgia, but we didn't just fall off the turnip truck. They could be mass murderers like the Manson family, for all we know. There are women serial killers these days who help lure the girls. Sometimes they even do the killing—and enjoy it!"

"Quick, call your uncle. I wonder if he's heard of them." Sirena fumbled with the card to read the name of the agency. "It says Blanchette Casting. I'll bet Peter Churchill's famous as all get-out!" she squealed.

Amelia dialed her uncle's number. His secretary said he was taking a meeting and couldn't be disturbed. Amelia stuffed her phone into her backpack.

Sirena finished the last spoonful of her sundae, scraping the pool of chocolate syrup from the bottom of the parfait dish. "We'll try later. Let's hit the rest of Hollywood Boulevard before it gets too late."

They forged down the street, constantly stopped by someone who wanted to sell them something or get something from them.

"Spare change?" asked a guy in battle fatigues. He carried a sign scrawled with "I fought for you. Now it's your turn to feed me."

Sirena and Amelia stuffed two dollars in his cup and scurried past him.

The man shouted out to them, "I'd sure like to eat them sweet Georgia peaches you got on your chest. I'll bet they're juicy!"

The girls almost skipped with excitement on the Hollywood Walk of Fame, stepping on the coral-pink terrazzo stars embedded on a charcoal-gray background in the sidewalk. They trod over the name of Grace Kelly, complete with a movie camera symbol etched in brass.

"One day people are going to walk all over my name," Sirena said, jumping from star to star.

"One day I'm afraid people are going to walk all over *me*. Hey, you already do!" Amelia gave Sirena a little poke.

"Let's try to finish looking at the stars on the sidewalk. I want to find my all-time favorite, Preston Cooper," Sirena said.

"He's not listed in the guidebook. Even though there are thousands of stars along the Walk, it says they've still got space for more people, so maybe he'll eventually get one."

They ambled down the fabled sidewalk, eyes glued to the ground.

"I hope they don't run out of room when it's my turn. Oh, excu-u-u-u-se me! I just stepped on Marilyn Monroe's star. I absolutely love her!" Sirena gushed.

"She died young, so she'll be a hottie forever!" Amelia said.

"I want to get a Constance Award statuette from one of the souvenir shops along here. And let's not forget to find out what your uncle knows about Peter Churchill."

"Wasn't his English accent the bomb? I wonder if he knows any British rock bands," Amelia said.

"Let's buy my award, and then we'll head over to Peter's hotel. We passed by it on our way here. This might be my big break!" Sirena lowered her sunglasses and looked intently into Amelia's eyes. "First I'll be a model and then a famous actress. There have been a few crossovers, but it's time for a new generation."

Sirena walked into a souvenir shop. She gazed at the movie memorabilia stacked from floor to ceiling: crew jackets, posters, magnets, and shot glasses decorated with movie images. A line of tourists snaked around the shop, waiting to buy a personalized model of a Hollywood Walk of Fame Star.

"Want to get our names together on a star for posterity? I'll pay," Amelia asked.

"No, I'll wait for the real thing. But I *will* bring home a Movie Constellation Award for now." Sirena located the plastic replicas with plaques for Best Friend, Best Dog, and Lead Actor. She examined a nine-inch Lead Actress statue and shrieked, "This one's so cool!" She flipped the Constance Award upside down to find the price tag and then checked the money in her wallet. "They've got to be kidding. Fifteen dollars?"

"Why don't you get a smaller one for eight bucks or a miniature for three dollars that collapses when you push the button on the bottom?"

"No, this will be my souvenir of our trip. I'll put it on my nightstand and wish on it each and every night before I go to sleep."

"Do you have room with all those photos of Preston Cooper from magazines you framed? In most of them, he's sucking face with some hot starlet," Amelia said.

"I can dream, can't I? There's room for everything I want. We can dream together. Hey, let's get over to the hotel for my audition. I've heard traffic around here in the afternoon is a lot worse than back home."

They left the shop and headed to the parking lot. "I know I'll get a star on Hollywood Boulevard. And my hand-and footprints will be in cement in the courtyard of a famous theater too! You'll be right there with me at the ceremonies," Sirena said.

"Maybe they'll ask me to put my brush in cement since I'm always fixing your hair!"

"Groucho Marx made an imprint of his cigar, and Roy Rogers had his horse Trigger step up, so why not?"

Amelia handed the ticket to the parking attendant, wondering if she had to give a tip after such an expensive fee. Sirena put on her sunglasses to lessen the glare of the afternoon sun. She had noticed that people in California wear their shades most of the time, both day and night, and often indoors.

Amelia's uncle's red Mustang swerved into the parking lot from Hollywood Boulevard.

"I hope he wasn't joyriding all this time. Uncle Abram told me to make sure the valet's a real one because he had a friend whose car was swiped from a restaurant by a guy who wore a red jacket and didn't even work there."

"It looks fine. Get in and let's go before we're too late," Sirena said with an edge stripping the Southern bloom off her voice.

Amelia tipped the guy fifty cents, feeling that it wasn't his fault everything was so expensive in L.A. "He didn't even say thank you." She pouted, and then Sirena mimicked her, which made her smile again.

They drove down Highland and turned right onto Sunset Boulevard. "We're going to know this road as well as Peachtree Street back home by the time we leave here," Amelia said. They passed a small freestanding shop with a huge cookie on the roof. "I read in the guidebook that this is the first Famous Amos cookie store. How cool that there is a guy named Wally Amos who makes the best chocolate-chip cookies ever! I thought it was a made-up name like Betty Crocker or Aunt Jemima."

Sirena's eyebrows arched. "You mean there isn't really a Betty Crocker? Who made that Easy Bake Oven we used to play on?"

"I can't believe I finally know something that you don't! I'll enjoy this moment while it lasts." Amelia turned up the radio and swiveled her head from side to side, trying to sightsee while she navigated toward the hotel.

The road was lined with trendy clothing boutiques and restaurants with outdoor tables that dotted the sidewalks. They saw a fast-food joint in a long silver train car under the shadow of a massive billboard on Sunset. Preston Cooper's dazzling smile spilled across the enormous poster.

Sirena let out a long sigh and said, "My face is going to be right up there too! Maybe I'll star in a movie with Preston Cooper one day."

Sirena's guidebook explained that outdoor signs along the curving boulevard were called "ego boards" because they were plastered with the faces of movie or recording stars who probably frequently drove down Sunset. She flipped through the pages to find out if Preston Cooper lived nearby.

The girls spotted the black windowless façade of The Comedy Store. They recited the names of famous comedians scrawled in chalky white paint on the front of the building, including Jay Leno and Lillie Tomlin.

On a hillside above Tower Records, one of the most famous restaurants in Los Angeles loomed like the Emerald City of Oz. Sirena said, "I read about Spago in the movie magazines. All the stars hang out there, eating duck pizza and sipping martinis. Do you think your uncle and Nicole will take us for dinner? I'm dying to go there."

"They've always got somewhere to go at night, but maybe they'll give us his credit card so we can eat by ourselves. I'll ask him. They say the pizza is much better than my favorite chain, Pizza Pan Party," Amelia said.

"You've got a lot to learn, girl! I hear the pizza is unbelievable, but you don't go there just for the fabulous food. You go there to see and be seen," Sirena said.

"They'll be looking at *you*, that's for sure."

"I'm going to dress up and mingle with celebrities. That's where Madonna and Michael Jackson went to an after-party when she did that number imitating Marilyn Monroe dripping in furs and diamonds. Remember? That's why it's called an after-party. *After* an awards ceremony!"

"I'm not dumb. Of course I remember. I had to watch you standing on my bed singing and wiggling your butt along with her while you used my bath towel as your mink stole. That's when Madonna was a platinum blonde."

"I was good, wasn't I?" Sirena struck a pose with one arm stretched above her head and her other on her hip.

"You were freakin' awesome, Sirena! Like always."

"One day everyone's going to know my name." Sirena said, seductively puckering her lips in the passenger car mirror.

They passed the rest of the retail establishments on Sunset. As they headed west, the street changed to a residential boulevard lined with mansions, many shrouded in thick hedges. When they drove by a stark white modern house, Sirena said, "Way too cold-looking for me. I'd rather have loads of statues and crystal chandeliers in an Italian villa."

"When was the last time you ever saw an Italian villa?"

"I've seen pictures of them when we were eating at Pasta Mama in Atlanta with my folks. I'm not a hick like you are," Sirena retorted, nudging Amelia's arm.

"Gee, thanks! Who's the one who's got the rich uncle who lets us ride around in his car and stay in his mansion with a bowling alley and an indoor swimming pool?" A tear collected on Amelia's freckled face. "And why'd you hit me?"

Sirena blew her a kiss and wiped the tear from her damp cheek. "Forgive me, honey? It was a love pat."

Amelia turned to smile at her.

"Don't look at me. Drive!" Sirena shrieked.

Amelia swerved into the palm-lined driveway of the glamorous hotel. A cute, suntanned valet quickly opened her car door. "How long will you be staying with us, miss?"

"Not long enough, I can tell you right now," Sirena answered.

"We're here to see a friend, Peter Churchill. He's in a casita," Amelia told the young man. "Does that mean he can't afford to stay in the main building?"

"Miss, the casitas at the hotel are some of our finest accommodations. Why don't you stop at the desk, and they'll help you locate your friend. Enjoy your visit."

He escorted Sirena out of the car and then drove away.

"Do you think we're dressed okay for a place like this?" Amelia asked Sirena. She spotted a girl about their age in a black miniskirt with loads of gold chains around her neck, getting into a sports car.

Then a striking brunette handed her ticket to the valet. She smoked a long, dark cigarette held by two perfectly manicured fingers dramatically poised skyward. Her jeans were strategically stained white at the knees and had little striped holes.

"At least our jeans aren't shredded," Amelia said.

Sirena and Amelia strolled along the red carpet up the steps to the entry of the hotel that was bordered by a profusion of hydrangeas. They waited in line at the marble counter manned by a cadre of people in crisp jackets. Finally they reached the front of the line.

"How may I help you, young ladies?" the clerk asked.

"We're here to see Peter Churchill," Sirena replied.

The man checked his computer screen and then punched an extension on the phone. "Who should I say is here?"

"His model Sirena and her hairstylist."

"Mr. Churchill, sorry to disturb you. Your guests, Miss Sirena and another young lady, are here for you."

Sirena smiled at getting top billing.

"Yes, I'll have them wait in the lobby." He turned to the pair and said, "Mr. Churchill will be here in a few minutes. May I get you something to drink while you wait?"

"No, it's okay, thanks." Sirena headed for a large round banquette, a velvet donut in front of the doors to the ballrooms. She sat with her spine straight, and Amelia plopped down next to her on the tufted circular bench.

"I would have liked a Coke. You never even asked me." Amelia pouted and scooted to the opposite side of the bench. She was beginning to feel the pain of being invisible next to a beautiful woman.

They watched the steady stream of well-heeled people entering and leaving the hotel. After a few minutes, Peter appeared from a long hallway. He gave Sirena and Amelia a kiss on each cheek, European style. "Would you girls like something to drink?"

"Yeah, a Coke," Amelia said, shooting a look at Sirena.

"The restaurant is right around the corner." They walked down the hall.

"Afternoon, Mr. Churchill," the hostess at the hotel bar said in a honeyed voice.

"We'll just stay in the bar area."

They were shown to a leather banquette in the intimate cocktail lounge. The afternoon sunlight poured into the next room from the wall of windows that overlooked the garden where countless entertainment deals had been crafted. Peter motioned for the teens to glide into the booth, and then he scooted next to Sirena.

"What can I get you, Mr. Churchill?" the waiter asked.

"I'll have a British Pimm's Cup, and these two beauties will have 'Atlanta's finest,' Coca-Cola."

Amelia wore a wide grin from being called a beauty and the joke about her favorite soft drink.

Right after the drinks were served, Gretchen Blanchette arrived. She slid in next to Amelia, reaching across her to give Peter a peck on each cheek. She pulled an advertising layout from her tote bag. "Here's the magazine two-page spread. There's an older couple on one page with a car that's loaded with extras, and the facing page has the stripped-down version with the younger twosome."

Sirena leaned over Amelia to get a better look. "Cool. Just think, I'll be standing right where you have a magic marker drawing." She stared with fascination at the mock-up spread across the cocktail table as if it were the *Mona Lisa.*

The waiter stood nearby waiting for Sirena to finish inspecting the ad layout. Gretchen smiled and said, "Nothing for me. I'm due at Mid-Wilshire and traffic's a bitch. Sorry, Peter, but I've got to run. Sirena, leave your contact info before you go."

Amelia sipped her soft drink and loudly munched on chips and dip that had instantly appeared even though Peter hadn't ordered them. Sirena didn't touch a bite, never taking her eyes off him. While Amelia shoveled huge scoops of the dip, she only saw the back of her friend's head.

Gretchen blew an air kiss to Peter and maneuvered out of her seat. On her way to the door, she stopped to talk to a woman with thick chestnut hair who was facing away from the group's table. The glamour girl turned around to wave to Peter.

Amelia banged on Sirena's knee under the table. "Oh my God, can you believe that Gretchen's actually talking to my favorite model with the most fabulous hair? I've got to get her autograph," Amelia said excitedly, fishing through her purse for a scrap of paper.

Peter reached across the table and patted her freckled arm. "Lovey, there's one thing you must learn if you're going to be in this town. You've got to act like you belong. Celebrities are everywhere, and it's very uncool to go mental every time you see one."

Sirena was proud that she hadn't even blinked when Amelia pointed out the gorgeous woman. Sirena instinctively knew this was going to be her world, and she would figure out how to become a part of it. She was sure the top model was wondering who was the pretty blonde sitting with Peter Churchill.

"Down the hatch! Let's get a few photos of my little Scarlett O'Hara." He signaled to the waiter for the check.

"But Scarlett was brunette," Amelia said.

Sirena shot her a look that said it all.

When the bill arrived, Peter patted his pockets and then the top of his head for his reading glasses. In an instant, the server arrived with a tray full of assorted eyeglasses.

"Now that's why I love this place," Peter said, selecting a pair of readers with the proper strength. "Thanks, lovey. You're absolutely brilliant."

The trio left the intimate cocoon of the bar and emerged into the airy lobby. They walked down a hallway and exited onto a meandering garden path.

The late-day sun filtered through the palms, and walls of hibiscus and bougainvillea bloomed in a rainbow of colors. Sirena and Amelia followed Peter down the walkway to his separate suite.

Amelia whispered, "I see what that car park guy was talking about. This looks like Peter has his own house here."

Peter opened the door and walked in, kicking off his loafers. His bare feet sank into the plush carpet. Sirena sat on a wingback chair in the living room of the grand suite. She unfastened her sandals and pushed them neatly under the chair. Amelia froze slack-jawed at the entryway. It was the most beautiful hotel room she had ever seen— much nicer than her living room at home.

"Come in. I won't bite," Peter said.

Amelia circumnavigated the room. She wandered into the huge bedroom and peeked at the Carrara marble in the master bath. She opened the door to a full bathroom off the main sitting area and finally landed on the couch facing the fireplace.

"Let's get started. Sirena, I'm going to take a few shots of you inside with artificial lighting, and then we'll go into the garden to catch the golden light when the sun lowers a bit. Stand next to the fireplace."

Peter went to the bedroom and returned with a large metal case with his gear. He pulled out a camera and looked through the viewfinder. He lowered his aim and frowned. "Amelia, you're in my frame."

She moved to a chair to try to get out of the shot.

"No good. You're still there, lovey. In fact, why don't you give us a few minutes so I can work with Sirena alone. Go to the gift shop and pick out a few souvenirs—a couple of hotel T-shirts. Tell them to charge it to me."

Sirena nodded to Amelia that it was okay. Amelia's mouth drooped in disappointment, like a wilted flower. "I'll be back in about ten minutes, y'all." She closed the door behind her.

"I want to make a few photographs of your profile. Sit in that chair by the window. One side needs to be in shade, and I'll highlight the other." Peter danced around her and then clicked off a few shots. Sirena tried to suppress a giggle and managed to muster a seductive smile with her chin down and her eyes beckoning. He pulled a print from the film pack. Sirena had never seen a professional instant-print camera before, larger than the ones for sale at her drugstore at home. Peter tossed the photos on the table and snapped a few more.

"Can I see them?" Sirena asked, getting up from the chair.

"Not until I finish. Let's move into the bedroom. Go ahead and stretch out on the bed."

"Uh, I don't think so." Sirena crossed her ankles together and pressed her back against the seat.

"You dirty girl! I just want to get your hair falling down your shoulders against a neutral background. Go ahead. Don't tell me you're one of those difficult types who can't take direction. I thought you were keener than that."

Sirena suddenly felt stupid, fearing she was beginning to lose her chance to be a model. She slowly entered the bedroom and sat on the chaise. Peter motioned to her to recline on the bed. She rested on her elbow on the beige silk duvet, sinking into the plush down.

"I think the writing on your T-shirt is distracting. If I show these test shots to the agency, it might turn them off." He tossed her a skimpy tank top with the hotel's logo embroidered on the front.

"But you sent Amelia out to get us some T-shirts. Look, if you're trying to get me to take my top off, why don't you come out and just ask."

"I must admit that I'd love to see what's under that awful stretchy thing. Why in God's green earth do you have graphics of fruit plastered across your beautiful breasts?"

"Georgia peaches *are* the sweetest and don't show their tits just because some sleazy old guy asks them to."

"Ouch, I don't know which hurts worse—being called 'sleazy' or 'old.'" Peter retreated to the living room and gathered the heap of test shots.

Sirena followed close behind and hunted for her shoes under the chair.

"Session's over. These photos look super. Gretchen will call you in the morning to tell you about your wardrobe and the location of the ad shoot. She'll courier the contracts to you later tonight. Good job, Sirena. You'll do just fine. You can bring Amelia with you, but tell her to try to be cool."

Sirena smiled and picked up her purse. She grabbed the bottom of her cropped T-shirt and flashed Peter a quick glimpse of her spectacular breasts. "I'll show them when *I* decide to. See you on the set, lovey." She laughed as she made her exit from the casita.

Sirena caught up with Amelia talking on the lobby phone in an alcove, with two shopping bags stuffed with items from the gift shop. "Okay, I know we're darned lucky to be alive," Amelia said. She waved to Sirena. "No, I didn't ask Peter Churchill if he knows you. Who hasn't heard of Abram Geller?" Looking over her friend from head to toe, Amelia said, "Yes, we're just fine, Uncle, and so is your car."

"I got it!" Sirena bubbled.

"I think she got the job. Not bad for her first day in Hollywood. Have a great time at the screening tonight, and we'll see you in the morning." Amelia replaced the phone in its cradle, and she and Sirena did a happy dance in the posh hotel lobby.

12

CHARLIE &
FRANCINE

"WHY IN THE HELL do I have to go to Vegas?" Coop asked, months before *Big House, Little Lady* was released in the theaters.

"Because you're going to get the Star of the Galaxy award, that's why," Charlie said. "It's not like it's the first time you've been to Cinema Exhibition Expo."

"That's all I really want to do—sit in a room with thousands of guys who sell popcorn across the country."

"Putting butts in seats is what it's about. Now they've got to be seats that rock, recline, and vibrate!" Charlie said. "Distribution is an important link in the film marketing chain."

"I know. I worked with a great exhibition president in the past, but I haven't made a movie with Nina's studio in about ten years," Coop said.

"You'll be happy with our team at Silverlake. We'll get a lot of press on *Big House, Little Lady* if you make an appearance at CE Expo. We'll even throw a dinner in your honor for all three thousand attendees. We'll be the only one because the rest of the majors have cheaped out and only do snacks and cocktails. Trust me, your award will be the most significant one given during the convention."

"If it's good for the picture, then I'll do it. Who else is being honored?" Coop asked.

Charlie slicked back her dark hair, tucking a loose tendril into the twist at the nape of her neck. "Let's see … Harold Dern from Phoenix is being named Exhibitor of the Year, and Sirena's getting the Leading Lady of the Century award."

"Okay, I'll go but I want separate flights for her and me. And make sure you remember that I only fly in the latest jets. Give her a prop plane, but she's not going with me."

"No problem. It's a short flight, but I'll have my assistant call you in a few days and find out what you want to eat on board. Just name it."

"Just make sure they serve her crow," Coop said.

A private jet carrying Preston Cooper buzzed the Las Vegas strip before it landed at Wiggins Field. The studio allowed Sirena to travel on the corporate Lear, and they had to hire a special plane for Coop. He cajoled the pilot into letting him take over the controls for most of the forty-five-minute flight from Burbank Airport. The pilot was accustomed to celebrity passengers who owned their own planes. It was no wonder to him why they didn't use their own aircraft because the fuel, even on a short flight, was exorbitant by the average person's standards. To a star it was pocket change, but most preferred to have the studio pick up the tab. Charlie had arranged that Coop would only have to appear at a dinner in the Grand Ballroom of the Arch de Triumph Hotel and then at a thirty-minute press conference afterward.

The weeklong convention in Las Vegas brought together movie theater chains and independent theater owners to sample the upcoming product from the studios and production houses. The convention scheduled a nonstop parade of stars, national and international speakers from movie studios, and an exhibition trade show that displayed every type of gadget and junk food. In an attempt to elevate the event beyond a run-of-the-mill trade show, Cinema Exhibition Expo featured a closing ceremony.

The titles of the awards were designed to entice the stars and movie executives to appear in Las Vegas. The celebrities usually showed up, even though it meant making a few glib remarks to a banquet room the size of a football field. They had to glad-hand with exhibitors from around the country who were thrilled to be in the mere presence of a real movie star. Some of the awards sounded serious, and others were trumped up, such as Moviegoers' Favorite Film of the Year and Male Star of Tomorrow.

Arthur and the rest of the Silverlake marketing department had huddled in Camelot with the President of Distribution, Richard Riggins. They had brainstormed how to get the most bang for their buck out of Cinema Exhibition Expo, conspiring to lure their two estranged stars to the convention. To the team's consternation, Coop and Sirena had avoided one another like they were each tuberculosis carriers after the wrap of the movie.

Richard said, "The creative department's got enough powerful clips from the dailies to string together a reel for Cinema Exhibition Expo. The director, Jack Wesson, is just starting postproduction, so we don't have much final footage of *Big House*. We can throw in a score from the studio's music library until the soundtrack is finished."

"The movie's still on schedule for a domestic release in August. We'll have to scramble to be ready for the international market at the Normandy Film Festival a month later," Charlie said, flipping through the flow chart.

Richard scrolled down the distribution release schedule on his tablet. "Jack's insisting on opening late summer after most of the action blockbusters have petered out. I think we should wait for the lull between Thanksgiving and Christmas that puts us closer to the awards ceremonies."

"From the footage I've already seen, *Big House* is going to sweep the Movie Constellation Awards this year. Our biggest worry right now is how we're going to get Coop and Sirena to show up at the same place at the same time in Las Vegas," Charlie added.

"What's happening with the Cinema Exhibition Expo? Okay, people, think about how to convince Coop and Sirena to go to Vegas! What's the bait?" Arthur asked.

Gabe's face lit up. "How about Star of the Galaxy for him? Not female or male, as they usually do for Star of the Year, but just the biggest of them all that encompasses both sexes."

"I think he'll go for it," Arthur said. "Good thinking, Gabe. Keep it up and you might get Charlie's job."

Gabe glanced at Charlie and shrugged his shoulders. She flashed him a quick smile, pleased that he was beginning to have some ideas of his own and not merely executing hers. She had been taught that the sign of a good executive is to groom an eventual successor. Charlie hoped that she, too, would move up the corporate ladder one day.

Richard lightly jabbed Gabe's arm. "Maybe I should get you in my department. We could use you in Distribution."

"Glad to help out, but I'm afraid Charlie's stuck with me."

"How could I get along without you?" Charlie said playfully. "Let's get back on track. Sirena's award has to be special and still not compete with Coop's. How about naming her the Leading Lady of the Century. This would celebrate her beauty, something that mainly leading ladies possess. No one has gotten it before because we just made it up, so that should appeal to her sense of vanity. Our product sponsor tie-in has agreed to share the cost of the main event."

"Done!" Arthur gave a thumbs-up. "Richard, get on the horn and make the arrangements with Cinema Exhibition Expo. Charlie, make sure that Coop and Sirena are on board. Why's everybody still standing around?"

Charlie knew that if anyone could get Coop to do something, it was his publicist. Every appearance that involved the star had to be approved by Francine Darten. She was his gatekeeper.

Charlie passed by Gabe's desk on her way into her office. "Empress Darten is on the line," he said.

"It only took her forty-eight hours to get back to me. Okay, patch her through." Charlie picked up the receiver. "Hey, girlfriend. I was just talking about you. Is Coop being a good boy these days?"

"Yeah, he's just fine. What's up?" Francine spoke into her speakerphone, her voice sounding hollow like she was in a tunnel. She leaned back with her spike heels propped on her desk.

"Cinema Exhibition Expo is coming up, and we want to make *Big House, Little Lady* the top draw. We can be part of the closing ceremony, *if* we get Coop to commit to an appearance."

"You know how he feels about the convention. Ever since they had that movie cowboy rope a calf at a luncheon, Coop's not very high on it. Especially when the poor guy got kicked in the nuts. No livestock demonstrations for *Big House*, okay?" Francine said.

"We just heard they want to name Coop as the Star of the Galaxy. That's the biggest award any actor has ever gotten," Charlie said.

"Will Sirena be there?"

"We're pretty sure that she will, but we'll keep them separate except for sitting on the dais at the dinner. We can stick the director and a few costars between them. Coop can be saved for last as the grand finale. Or if you think it's better for him to go first, it's up to the two of you."

"I'll run it by him. It might be best if he goes first because then he can leave, saying he's got something important to do."

"We would like him to stick around for the press, but perhaps we can host a VIP reception for a few top members of the media at a hospitality suite, and he would be the only star present. How's that sound?" Charlie asked. She clicked her pen open and shut, waiting for the response she wanted to hear.

"The whole thing smacks of steer wrestling to me, but I'll let you know," Francine said.

"Okay. Give me a call back *pronto*, so we have time to make this an event Coop will enjoy," Charlie said cheerfully.

"Not to worry, sweetheart. This sounds like a win-win for Coop," Francine said.

13
COOP &
SIRENA

AFTER A FLURRY OF PHONE CALLS, Coop agreed to make the appearance at the Cinema Exhibition Expo. The Grand Suite at the Arc de Triomphe Hotel in Las Vegas was reserved for him. With a spectacular view of the half-scale model of the Eiffel Tower outside his window, it was one of the most luxurious suites in the city filled with glamorous gambling palaces.

Francine accompanied Coop in the private elevator that led directly to the penthouse. It was programmed as an express run, so no gawking tourists would have the good fortune of riding with one of Hollywood's biggest movie stars.

Francine had been at Cinema Exhibition Expo all week to ensure her clients were being well treated by the press. Charlie was slated to arrive at the hotel, accompanied by Jamaal Kenter, who was assigned to guard Coop during the closing ceremonial dinner.

The manager of the hotel joined Coop and Francine in the elevator. "I hope you're going to be pleased with this suite," he said.

"We'll see soon enough. Silverlake Pictures made all of the arrangements, right?" Francine asked.

"To the last detail."

"I assume they informed you of Coop's per diem. It should be transferred to his credit line at the casino. We'll be here for only one night, so please make sure this is done as soon as possible," Francine said.

The manager inserted the room key and then swung open the door with a flourish. The crystal chandelier sparkled like a constellation above the dining room table surrounded by a dozen chairs. Francine conducted a quick inspection trip around the place, trailed by the manager who enumerated the amenities. "A Jacuzzi in one bath and a bidet in the other."

"Francine, scratch the request for a bidet from my personal travel profile," Coop said.

"Did Mr. Cooper's exercise equipment arrive yet? We specifically requested that it be assembled in the room adjoining this suite."

"Yes, everything is in place as was relayed to us by the movie studio. If there's anything we can do to make your stay here more enjoyable, just let me know. Here's my card with my personal cell number." The manager backed out of the room.

Coop walked into the living room and plopped down on the overstuffed couch without bothering to slip off his shoes. His eyelids drooped shut, closing off the others.

"I'll leave you alone for a while. I've got to meet with Charlie, and then I'll give you a buzz, sweetheart." Francine snatched a chocolate truffle from the silver tray on the coffee table next to a sweeping arrangement of white orchids and roses. She softly shut the door to the suite.

With the click of the lock, Coop's deep blue eyes popped open. He walked to the window festooned with brocade drapes and pulled them back to reveal the gleaming replica of the Eiffel Tower on the horizon.

It had only been two years since he and Sirena had occupied a room with a view of the real tower in the capital of France. They had been on a trip to Europe to promote the international release of his film *Mad about Paris*. It was a frothy romantic romp, a role the public loved to see the handsome leading man play.

Coop and Sirena had been transported from Charles De Gaulle Airport to a grand old hotel that was situated on one of the most beautiful plazas in Paris, with an Egyptian granite obelisk at the base of the Champs-Élysées. Their driver explained that the plaza had once been the scene of a bloodbath when spectators were trampled during the fireworks display at the celebration the marriage of Louis XVI to Marie-Antoinette near the sculpture of Louis XV. During the French Revolution, the statue was toppled, along with the heads of the royal couple on the very same spot.

"I hope the Parisian press gives us better treatment than that after they see our film!" Coop said.

The chauffeur navigated through the stream of traffic, racing around the slender tower covered with hieroglyphics that replaced the fallen statue. He arrived at the entrance of the hotel.

Coop and Sirena whirled through the revolving door, out of the bustle of the street, into the sedate Louis XV elegance with gleaming marble. They spotted Francine sitting in the lobby, sipping a cup of tea with her assistant Mercedes Le Blanc along with the hotel manager, Jacques Lefevre. Central casting couldn't have selected a more debonair gentleman to serve at the helm of the venerable five-star palace. After the usual pleasantries, the manager accompanied the two stars to the penthouse. Coop had told Francine and Mercedes to stay put, certain he and Sirena were in good hands with the head of the hotel.

"I think you will be pleased with the Royal Suite," M. Lefevre said. "It seems to be a favorite of people in the American cinema."

The door to the suite swung open. A plush velvet couch faced the marble fireplace, and the dining table could accommodate twelve guests. Rich brocades sumptuously draped the windows revealing a spectacular view of the Eiffel Tower. Then M. Lefevre led them through the suite to the bedroom with a canopy similar to the private royal compartments in palaces and the regal bed they shared at home. The bedroom included a walk-in closet with ample room for endless wardrobe changes for public appearances.

"I trust this is to your satisfaction."

"Very cool," Sirena said.

Coop grunted his assent while nibbling on his wife's swanlike neck.

"Enjoy your stay." The manager left the couple in the bedroom and discretely let himself out.

Coop and Sirena took one look at each other and then dove onto the satin duvet. Sirena said, "It's fucking gorgeous! I can't wait for Amelia to see it. She said she's going to do my hair in a French twist."

"Let's make good use of this great big bedroom," Coop said.

"Sounds good, but I think there are better things to do while we're here—shopping! But first let's go look outside on the terrace to get the lay of the land," Sirena said.

She grabbed Coop's arm and walked into the living room, flinging open the doors that let in a breeze mixed with traffic smells and the scent of roses. The suite was situated on one of the front corners of the hotel facing the plaza, with a limestone balustrade surrounding an enormous private terrace that wrapped around the façade.

Sirena leaned over the stone railing, enjoying the warmth of morning sunshine on her face. "How much do you think they paid for this place a night?"

"Francine told me the studio gets a deal, but the rack rates aren't even published. It's thousands, I've heard. Enjoy it, babe. There's more to come when we get to London for the Royal Premiere."

"I can't wait to make a dent in the designer shops! Maybe I'll buy Amelia a silk scarf from Hermès when she and I hit the stores. It would be nice to get her something special. She does so much for me."

"Just go downstairs to the front desk each morning and tell them you want my daily draw. Have a ball, and then charge the rest. I think it's time that we check out that bed," he said. "Ever been French kissed before in France?"

"Oh, *monsieur*, such a bold question!"

"Come here and let me show you how it's done," he said, cupping her breasts. Then he led her by her slim waist to the bed.

Sirena climbed onto the plush bed, scattering the mountain of pillows in all directions. She bent over Coop, straddling his jeans while pulling off her halter. He kissed her breasts, flicking her nipples with his tongue. He slowly worked his way up to her mouth. In a long, deep kiss, she didn't know if she was dizzy from the jet lag or from his overwhelming embrace. Coop pushed her aside playfully and unzipped his jeans. He kicked off his loafers, and she yanked down his pants in a flourish, tossing them across the room.

"Did you know we can see the Eiffel Tower in this room too?" Sirena asked.

He glanced down with satisfaction at his cock that was pointed skyward. "Well, come climb aboard and I'll give you one hell of a ride to the top."

14
CHARLIE & THE
FIELGOODS

C HARLIE WATCHED ARTHUR AND TEENI approach the red carpet at
the entrance to the theater on the night of the Movie Constellation
Awards. Along the way, he stopped to shake the hands of other movie
executives and plant kisses on female stars he had worked with at
Silverlake Pictures. He never missed an opportunity to smooch with
a somewhat willing woman. Teeni had warned him when he lingered
too long with an Italian bombshell, "Hey, no tongues, Arturo!"

The sultry actress laughed and said in a thick accent, "Believe me,
signora, he is all yours. *Ciao!*"

That wasn't the first time Charlie had seen Arthur get a little too
up close and personal with a woman other than his wife. Years before
when she had started working at Silverlake Pictures, her roommate,
Cindy, had invited her to a party at B-movie producer Ross Nelson's
estate, a palace in the heart of Beverly Hills. It was a fund-raiser for
the legalization of marijuana. Although Charlie had given up smoking
weed in college, it presented a perfect opportunity to get a good look

at the fabled mansion. The typical June-gloom mixture of fog and smog clung in the early-evening air.

Cindy's boyfriend, Sean Shannigan from Silverlake, bought the tickets to the party. She promised to leave Charlie's name on the guest list.

Charlie arrived in her old clunker. As she entered the lower gates of the mansion, she rolled down her window to speak to the guard who was eyeing her car with suspicion.

"Name, please?"

"Charlie Wallach from Silverlake Pictures."

"Says here that there's a Charlene Wallach on the list. Where is she? The invitation isn't transferable."

"No, I'm Charlene; Charlie's my nickname."

"May I see your ID?"

She fumbled in her purse and finally produced her driver's license with the name Charlene and her sports club membership card that said Charlie.

"Okay, you're fine. Enjoy the evening. The valet's up there." He nodded to the sprawling house on a hill.

Charlie gunned the engine. At the top of the winding driveway, vehicles were queued around a circle with a fountain in the middle. Finally she inched to the front of the line.

A female parking attendant surveyed the car. "We don't get many of these up here," she said.

"I should have one of those bumper stickers that says 'My other car is a Rolls,'" Charlie replied.

"Better watch out. I hear it's a jungle in there with lots of wolves and a few sharks in the pool. Here's your claim check, and have a good time."

Charlie approached the mansion that resembled a chateau with a beige limestone façade. At the massive door, a long-legged blonde with an impressive bustline checked the guest list one more time.

"Welcome to the estate, honey. The buffet will open at six thirty, and we'll watch a movie in about five minutes. Make yourself at home."

Charlie was surprised at the girl's friendliness to another female. A waiter passed by with skewers of lobster on a silver tray, and Charlie followed him into the heavily paneled den with a cloying hint of cigar smoke in the air. She nibbled on lobster while she scanned the crowd for Cindy and Sean.

Charlie wandered into the game room lit by a pair of elegant, antique stained glass lamps. She spotted the host wearing yards of gold chains displayed through his open-neck shirt. He was deeply engrossed in conversation with a striking woman dressed in cut-off jeans. Still no sign of Cindy.

One of the few brunette vixens in the room walked around announcing it was time for the movie to start. Her breasts were like overinflated balloons harnessed by a skimpy top. In contrast, Charlie felt she was dressed more like she worked in a bank than at a movie studio. She might as well have had the word "conservative" plastered across her normal-proportioned chest.

The crowd slowly drifted into a huge screening room. Rows of chairs began to fill with celebrities and civilians. Some people lingered at the bar, and others wandered around the vast property that could be seen from the expansive picture windows.

Charlie grabbed a seat and secured the two next to her with her purse and jacket, hoping Sean and Cindy would surface. After a few minutes, she had to relinquish the seats to a couple who glared at her for inconveniencing them. The lights dimmed and the credits for *Reefer Madness* rolled with the original title, *Tell Your Children.* In it, a high school principal, Dr. Carroll, warned parents at a PTA meeting about the dangers of marijuana. The audience at the Nelson Estate enjoyed the melodramatic 1930s film. Charlie detected a sweet and pungent smoky smell wafting through the room, and it wasn't from Ross's cigar.

The organizer of the fund-raiser thanked the audience for supporting the cause. He described the group's efforts to decriminalize
marijuana in all states. He listed their success in the battle to get pot
legalized for medicinal use to ease the side effects of cancer treatments.
Charlie looked around in the flickering light; Cindy and Sean were
still missing in action.

After a round of applause, the moviegoers dispersed like a swarm
of locusts to the dining room. They engulfed the massive buffet table
laden with platters of rare tenderloin and sushi artfully arranged like
a pair of red lips. Charlie snatched a few tidbits and then resumed her
hunt for her friends.

She asked the blonde who had greeted her at the front door, "Could
you see if Sean Shannigan from Silverlake Pictures and his date Cindy
have arrived yet?"

The girl ran her long pink fingernail along the list. She stopped
halfway down the first page and pointed to the checkmark next to his
name. "Yes, he's here—a party of two."

"Any idea where they might be?"

"Go out these doors and check by the pool area, cupcake. It's always
a hot spot."

"Thanks," Charlie said and looked longingly at the buffet as she
headed to the door at the back of the room. She walked onto the patio
filled with tables covered with green canvas umbrellas, feeling the glow
of portable heaters in the brisk summer evening air. At the edge of
the pool, girls in skimpy bikinis, with their long, cascading hair held
back by sunglasses perched on their heads, lounged under the heat
lamps. Their golden-tanned figures dotted the landscape, creating a
living sculpture garden of Aphrodites.

Charlie followed the path along the pool until she came to a massive hot tub surrounded with columns. Groups of women in the misty
water swam nude like water nymphs. Charlie spotted Cindy with

her legs wrapped around Sean in the waist-high water. Her exposed breasts glistened, and Charlie couldn't tell if Sean was wearing bathing trunks. Cindy held a plastic margarita glass while her other hand was busily submerged. They moved farther into the secluded area behind the waterfall that cascaded over an aqueduct.

Charlie hid behind a high hedge, hoping her friends hadn't seen her. Then a couple walked past her. The man looked familiar from the movie trade magazines, and the woman was obviously one of Ross's B-list bombshells.

"Kiddo, with a face like yours, there's got to be a part in one of our pictures for you," the man said to the starlet.

"Oh, Artie, do you really think so?" the woman cooed as they plunged into the water from the pool steps. His white buttocks shone like giant mushrooms, illuminated by subdued landscape lighting hidden in the foliage.

"I'll let you know in a few minutes." He pulled her closer to him and untied her string bikini top, liberating a pair of gigantic silicone floaters. "But first I'll show you why they call me Mr. Fielgood." Then he let fly her little leopard string bikini bottom that landed a few inches from Charlie's feet. Arthur looked at Charlie and said, "Let your hair down from that bun. There's plenty of room in here for one more, kiddo."

Charlie backed into a low sago palm in her attempt to escape. The sharp fronds poked through her slacks. She headed toward the tables, passing the trampoline with a nimble starlet bouncing in gravity-defying positions. Charlie marveled how the jumper could spread her legs so far apart and still land upright and smiling. She figured it must have taken years of practice.

A woman in a cocktail suit careened past Charlie, almost knocking her into a tiki torch. In a shrill voice that rose above the sound of the waterfall, Teeni Fielgood yelled, "Artie, I'll give you two minutes to get your ass over here! Come out, come out from wherever you are!"

15
CHARLIE &
TEENI

WHEN ARTHUR FIELGOOD ARRIVED at Silverlake Pictures as Charlie's boss, she prayed that he didn't remember her from his pool romp several years before at Ross Nelson's estate. She didn't think it was politically expedient to have seen her supervisor butt-naked in the act of *flagrante delicto*.

Office gossip linked Arthur to various movie stars. It was hard to imagine why, because he wasn't particularly handsome. Some said power is a strong aphrodisiac; others claimed that his member rivaled Milton Berle's legendary staff, and they weren't talking about the late comedian's stable of writers.

Teeni's temper was notorious, and she divorced five husbands before she snagged Arthur. Each was rumored to have been more successful than the last, but they didn't stay with her for long. People speculated she always wore couturier clothes because she didn't want to don anything that had been touched by another body, even her underwear. After knowing the difficult Hollywood wife for a while, Charlie

understood why the marketing team called "the clotheshorse" behind
her back. She particularly gravitated toward hues that complemented
her aubergine hair, a deep reddish-purple shade that her hairdresser
swore he would not use on any of his other clients.

In Teeni's inflated view of herself, she was an indispensable asset
to her husband. When it suited her, she accompanied him to business
dinners and screenings. At a dinner party at the Steps Dining Club and
Spa in Rome on the Via Condotti, she made her mark on the bastion
of elegance and tradition.

Marco Alessandro, head of the Italian office of Silverlake Pictures,
invited Arthur, Teeni, and Charlie to dinner.

Although the Hollywood studio paid the expenses, the principals
abroad lived in royal style. The managing directors of Silverlake Pictures
in each of the participating countries were chauffeured by private
drivers, dined only at the finest restaurants, and belonged to posh
private clubs—to entertain exhibitors, visiting filmmakers, and stars.

Charlie was excited about being on her first international business
trip. She and the Fielgoods rode together from their hotel, and the
driver delivered them promptly to the club at eight thirty. The doorman
greeted the group with a proper bow from the waist.

"We're joining Mr. Alessandro for dinner," Charlie said.

"He's in the Cigar Bar. Who shall I say has arrived?"

"His guests from Silverlake Pictures," Charlie said, following the
man up the wooden stairs to a tree-lined patio.

"I'm sorry, *signora*, the Cigar Bar is in the gentlemen's section of
the spa. You are welcome to wait in the Grand Salon." He pointed to a
room decorated like a jewel box in brocades and intricate mosaic tables.

Retreating to the salon, Charlie almost collided with Teeni, who
had started to climb the short staircase leading to the bar.

"What kind of old-fashioned, sexist bullshit do I have to put up
with in this country?" Teeni continued toward the outdoor space.

"Pardon, *signora*. I'm sure it would be possible to seat your party in the main dining room right away. It's our tradition that no lady has entered this bar area since its inception."

"Well, I'm from America, and we don't have such fucked-up rules. I can smoke my brains out if I want on the balcony back at our hotel down the street, but I'm not all that crazy about cigars, if you really want to know."

"What's all this fuss about cigars?" Marco asked as he emerged from the Cigar Bar, followed by two other Italian executives. "Teeni, you haven't changed a bit since I last saw you. You look beautiful, *bella*. I'm positively famished. Shall we? *Andiamo!*"

Her smile surfaced, and she took his arm as Marco led the group into the main restaurant. "Terribly sorry, but my wife, Angelica, will be here shortly. She's behind schedule. She had to take her own car because there wasn't time to send my driver back home to collect her."

The maître d' invited Teeni to take a seat, with Marco on her right and her husband on her left. Charlie was flanked by Marco's two associates.

As the cocktail orders were being taken, a woman in a chic suit with a Gucci shawl draped with flair arrived at the table. Sparkling with vitality, she rushed to her husband who rose to greet her. Angelica reached past Marco to extend her hand to Teeni, who kept her fingers tightly clasped in her lap. Angelica then adjusted her wrap, elegantly saving face.

"Teeni, forgive me for being late," Angelica said.

"You always do enjoy making an entrance. We haven't even gotten our drinks yet," Teeni said with a crooked smile. "Doesn't anyone have any pull around here?"

"Teeni, have anything you like," Marco replied smoothly.

"I'd like to go smoke with that bunch of bastards on the patio." She crossed her arms smugly.

After dinner, Marco suggested that he show his party the rest of the Steps Dining Club and Spa. They climbed the winding staircase and discovered a classical sculpture gallery at the top of the landing.

"This place just oozes with class and old money," Arthur said softly to Teeni.

"It certainly beats the hell out of the studio commissary," Teeni replied.

Etchings of elegant landscapes with cypresses lined the walls. The group took the elevator to see the swimming pool and spa surrounded by columns.

Arthur moved closer to Charlie and whispered, "A bit swankier than Ross Nelson's pool, wouldn't you say?"

Charlie swallowed hard. Trying to act as if she hadn't heard his comment, she scurried ahead to catch Marco's attention.

He explained to Teeni, "The food is marvelous, and I try to dine here as often as possible. Did you enjoy your meal, Charlene?"

"I prefer 'Charlie.' Yes, the angel hair pasta was memorable."

"The lobster *fra diavolo* wasn't too bad," Teeni added.

Arthur caught up with the threesome. "Charlie, how about a dip?"

"You know the breaststroke isn't my thing," she said.

"Let's go to the Cigar Bar and have a nightcap," Teeni suggested, elbowing Arthur.

"I've got international fires to put out with Marco regarding our release schedule, so I think it's time for you to call it a night," Arthur said. "Charlie, why don't you and Teeni head back to the hotel, and I'm going to stay and talk business with Marco and the guys for a while."

"I'd be glad to stay too, Arthur," Charlie offered.

"Kiddo, why don't you two gals run along? Teeni needs to get up bright and early to find something to wear to the Roman Premiere because her second suitcase still hasn't arrived."

"I simply can't bear to wear off-the-rack instead of couturier!" Teeni fumed. "Marco, can you get me in touch with a top designer?

A big one had better make room for me. I'm a size double zero, so it shouldn't take an atelier very long to whip up something in time."

"My assistant will ring your hotel in the morning. She will be at your disposal all day. I'm sure we can work something out for you, Teeni," Marco said.

"Make sure they have some silk that goes with my hair. There's no sense in wasting my precious time. The airline is going to pay for this through the nose."

Charlie and Teeni headed toward the exit. Teeni turned and said, "You're so lucky, Charlie. It really doesn't matter what you wear because no one is going to be looking at you. It's such a responsibility for me to bring a little Hollywood glamour to these dreary events."

"Yes, it must be an awesome burden," Charlie said with a lilt of sarcasm that didn't register with its target.

"I do it for Arthur. He really needs me to help him at these functions."

"*Ciao*. Please come again," the doorman said.

"When hell freezes over!" Teeni replied.

Charlie and Teeni ducked into the back seat of the limo.

"Where to?" the driver asked.

"Take us to our hotel and step on it!" Teeni commanded.

"Step on what, *signora*?"

"Oh never mind. *Fongool!* Just drive the car!" Teeni barked. "Hey, Charlie, bet you didn't know I speak fluent Italian."

16
COOP

O N THE NIGHT OF THE Movie Constellation Awards, Sirena's white stretch limo finally lumbered away to its parking spot somewhere in the bowels of Hollywood. After the long delay, Coop's vehicle pulled up to the drop-off area at the red carpet of the theater. He barely waited for it to come to a complete stop before he jumped out. The driver dashed around the passenger side to assist with the door, but he was too late.

An army of limousine drivers remained stationed, waiting for hours with their cell phones at the ready so they could be available when their clients wanted to leave the theater. The celebrity passengers were given claim tickets with numbers so the transportation team could coordinate the parade of limos after the event. Coop put the tag with 711 in his pocket.

"My lucky numbers. I won't be staying long at the Constellation Ball afterward, so be ready when they page you," Coop said.

He spotted Sirena on the red carpet at the mouth of the entrance to the theater. She posed next to oversized statues of Constance Awards for the demanding press photographers and television camera crews. Some shots were solos and others various suggestive pairings with Ethan Dean Traynor. The couple was bathed in the searing light of flashing cameras.

The rain had slowed down to a veil of mist. The forecasters had predicted it would totally subside by the time the three-hour ceremony ended. Traffic would be bad enough without the added nuisance of a downpour.

As Coop stepped onto the red carpet, commentator Judy Simmons swooped down on him like a vulture. Her thick, dark curls flew around her face when the wind picked up. She motioned to her cameraman to follow her as she approached the star. "Ladies and Gentlemen, he's finally here. Coop, how about a few words from the sexiest man in the world?"

"Judy, I'd love to, but I've got to keep moving. The show's about to start."

"Big star with places to go. Ignore me just as you did with your adorable little ex-wifey, Sirena."

"How nice to see you tonight, Judy. Have a great evening." He smiled for the cameras and headed for the entrance.

To the television camera, Judy said in a stage whisper, "The fall to the bottom is much harder than the climb to the top. Wasn't that red bow tie of his simply enough to make you gag?" She stuffed her thick index finger into her mouth.

The crowds in the bleachers shouted and waved wildly as he sprinted by.

"Coop, Coop, how about an autograph?"

"We love you, Coop!"

A sign caught his attention: "Sirena is bonkers. I'll take you anytime—anywhere!"

Coop stopped dead in his tracks seconds before he entered the building. He doubled back and then ran toward the bleachers. The fans screamed and clapped when he bent down and kissed the cheek of a young girl sitting on the side in a wheelchair. Her hands flailed in delight.

Coop saluted the throngs in the bleachers and then sprinted toward the theater entrance.

Francine trailed closely behind him, cursing her high heels. She was used to his impulsive actions. She thought, *Smart move. Tomorrow a clip of this kiss will show up on every channel across the country.*

Judy Simmons had witnessed the whole thing. She peered into the camera and said, "That little girl is so lucky to be sitting near the curb. She just got a kiss from the biggest movie star of all time. Coop really is a great guy, and he's great looking!"

The minute Coop stepped off the red carpet, handlers for the ceremony engulfed him. He checked his appearance in the large mirror in the lobby, as did every other star who walked past it. The ushers led him and Francine to the first row of the auditorium, the best seats in the house. An unfamiliar couple popped out of their chairs, relinquishing the prime spots to Coop and Francine.

The displaced pair in formal attire, seat-fillers, constituted an integral part of the telecast of the Movie Constellation Awards. Members of the awards staff volunteered to attend the ceremony to temporarily sit in stars' chairs when they went to the restroom or were presenting or accepting prizes. The television producers lived in dire fear of empty seats in their camera shots. The rules changed over the years about who could go to the star-studded event for free and get great access even if it was for ten-minute intervals. In the past, seat-fillers had been volunteers who were friends or relatives of Movie Constellation Association members or attractive young women in evening gowns who were selected for the job. Due to increased security, the selection policy tightened up and only staff members or their associates were offered the position.

Coop and Francine sat in the front of the center section. Sirena and Ethan were a dozen seats over on the end of the same row. A chill hung in the air between the former spouses. Other nominees and a smattering of studio heads occupied the first ten rows of the theater. Arthur and Teeni Fielgood took their places on the fifth row.

"Couldn't you get a better seat than this? What's the good of being the president of a division of a studio, for Chrissake?" Teeni whined.

"It's better than last year, and besides, we're in front of my counterpart from Premium Star Studios," Arthur said, waving to people he recognized sitting behind him in the auditorium.

"Last year we were in the third row. You're slipping, Artie."

"Teeni, third row on the side isn't nearly as good as fifth row center. We'll be in the camera shots much more often. Look who's around us: all the acting nominees," Arthur said.

"It's still farther back. But at least I'm next to him." She mustered a closed-mouth smile at the sexy male star sitting next to her.

In the front row, Coop stretched his long legs, trying to relax before the show started. He wondered if everyone back in Bent Branch, Texas, would be watching the telecast. Although they had taunted him when he was growing up, none of his former classmates could resist being interviewed by the tabloids, which were always trying to dig up dirt to sully his "Mr. Nice Guy" image.

As an adolescent, Coop was pegged as a quiet, brooding type. His schoolwork was mediocre, and he consistently ranked in the lowest percentile of his class. His mother arranged for tutors to improve his reading skills, and in general, school was hostile territory for Robby, young Robert Preston Cooper.

He possessed little aptitude for football, easily suffering from fatigue. Since Robby couldn't make the varsity team, he was appointed manager by his father and had to stay behind after the games and clean the equipment and close up the locker room. He thought being the coach's son wasn't all fun and games.

As part of his duties, he locked up the balls in the equipment closet and took to the showers after the team had finished washing up. While the other guys paraded around stark naked, Robby always made sure he was covered with a towel or a T-shirt.

When he was in the tenth grade, rumors spread like wildfire that he was gay. He never asked out any of the girls and occasionally went with a group of kids to the movies. Usually he kept to himself and studied for hours, trying to comprehend the homework assignments that sent him into a panic.

Before that, when he first hit puberty at around twelve, his mother had started taking him to a pediatrician in Austin, while everyone else went to Dr. Hughes, the local Bent Branch physician. By the next year he was feeling better and his grades improved slightly.

When he was a freshman in high school, his friend Travis came over to the house for lunch. The two boys settled in the den to watch a football game on television before they started on their math homework.

"Robby, whatcha got to drink around here?" Travis asked.

"The usual stuff. Whatcha want?"

"How 'bout a beer?"

"Cool with me, but Mom would have a hissy fit if she caught us drinking. Go check out the fridge and see what we've got. Bring me a soda pop. Help yourself," Robby said.

Travis ambled into the kitchen. He rooted around in the refrigerator and pulled back the panel on a plastic compartment on the door. He swaggered back into the room, waving a syringe full of liquid. "Hey, Hoss, what's this for? This box of shots has your name on it. Are you on dope or somethin'?" Travis asked.

"Hell no. What're you doing poking through other people's stuff?"

"You said to help myself, so I did. I didn't go looking for this shit. What is it?"

Robby tried to snatch the syringes, but Travis was too quick. The two boys raced around the kitchen. "It's for my allergies. I take allergy shots once a week. Got to give them to myself."

"What, you stick a needle in the butt?" Travis asked.

"Not in my butt—in my thigh. It's no big deal. I don't even feel it. My allergist in Austin says I need the shots every week. I can't go running back and forth all the time two hours away."

"So what are you allergic to?"

"Besides homework and you? Uh, I've got cedar fever. The whole area is loaded with cedar trees. Even when the pollen count isn't high around here, I've still got to keep taking my shots. They say it builds my immunity or something like that. And cats too."

"You don't even have a cat. So why didn't you never say anything about it? I don't see you sneezing or nothin'," Travis said while examining the plastic packet of needles.

Robby grabbed the syringes from his friend. "You'll contaminate them. Listen, no need to spread this around. People think I'm a big wuss as it is, so just forget it. Don't freak out. It's just allergies."

"Okay, forgotten," Travis said.

"Wait right here, and I'll get you a soda."

"I'd rather have a beer," Travis said, feeling the upper hand.

"*No problema*," Robby said, liberating a bottle from the cardboard six-pack in the fridge.

Robby constantly worried about his grades in high school. He had trouble concentrating, and his teachers often accused him of drifting off into daydreams. He couldn't always explain what was on his mind and often had to pause to collect his thoughts, which seemed to evaporate in midair.

There was one safe haven during his turbulent school day; he looked forward to Mr. Elkins's drama class because he could speak the lines without thinking. The words effortlessly floated in his mind.

Mr. Elkins walked down the rows of students at their desks, stopping to tap Robby on the shoulder. "Are you still with us, Mr. Cooper?"

"Yep, I was just …"

"And what do we say instead of 'yep' if we don't want to be typecast the rest of our lives as rednecks?" Mr. Elkins asked.

"Yes. Sorry, sir." Robby sat straighter in his seat.

"I want you kids to discover a world outside the dusty streets of Bent Branch. That's what being in the theatre can do for you. Not only acting in plays but also reading them and being transported by the language. When you're an actor, you can be anyone in the world. You can be brave or funny or sexy even if you're not in real life," Mr. Elkins said, broadly sweeping his hands.

A ripple of uncomfortable laughter ran through the room.

"Robby, I'm going to cast you as Willy Loman in *Death of a Salesman*. I want you to dig deep. When you're reading the script, find the part of yourself that evokes Willy's depths of despair. It can even be something minor, like not getting what you wanted for Christmas. We all have self-doubt and anguish that we can draw upon when we're crafting a character."

"But he's so old. I thought I'd get to play Happy or maybe Biff."

"Trust me, it's one of the greatest roles in the American theatre. One day you'll thank me for making you work this hard." Mr. Elkins returned to his desk and picked up Arthur Miller's 1949 Pulitzer Prize-winning script to read to the class.

Robby spent his rare free time working on drama practice with Mr. Elkins, time he stole from the tight schedule his father kept for him. The teacher always helped him find the subtle nuances of the passages that he couldn't decipher for himself but became clear when explained. The trick was to retain the text, to make the words stick in his brain.

After months of rehearsal, the review in the school paper lauded Robert Preston Cooper's portrayal of Willy Loman in *Death of a Salesman* as "a revelation dripping with pathos."

As a pleasant side effect of working with Mr. Elkins, Robby's history and English grades started to improve gradually. The letters on the pages weren't just confusing squiggles in a series of endless paragraphs.

Sometimes he found himself dreaming about becoming an actor. Robby wondered how he'd find a college that would accept him with such mediocre grades.

In his senior year, he heard about an open casting call in Austin for a Hollywood television show. Robert Preston Cooper figured it was his ticket to show business and his way out of small-town living.

Years later, Coop's so-called childhood friend Travis was interviewed by the *National Tell-Tale Magazine*. He described how he had confronted Coop about his drug use. He didn't say that he had found the syringe in the boy's parents' fridge, an unlikely place to hide illicit drugs, prescription or not. He told stories about how Coop was a loner, with only Travis as his best friend and confidant. He always had the feeling there was something strange about Coop, whom he referred to as Robby. Nevertheless, Travis boasted how he always believed his closest buddy would become famous one day.

17
COOP &
SIRENA

FRANCINE RAN TO CATCH UP with Coop at the Movie Constellation Awards when he pulled his act of kindness on the red carpet with the girl in the wheelchair. She wished she had thought of it, the perfect publicity stunt. He was always hugging a forlorn child who was in cancer treatment, or he was willing to stop at the scene of an accident to lend a hand. Francine told him that one of these days his Good Samaritan acts might bite him in the ass, but he swore he cared about people and couldn't turn his back on someone in need.

Coop and Francine had dashed through the theater past the ornate staircase to the doorway leading to orchestra seating. Even though the countdown clock was furiously ticking to begin the telecast, Coop paused to shake hands with the President of the Movie Constellation Association, Mitchell Franklin.

Mitchell had been a celluloid heartthrob in the 1940s and had enjoyed a long and stunning career. His good looks endured through the decades, and now a full head of distinguished silver hair was just as impressive as his wavy black locks had been when he was a young stud. Mitchell sported his signature, tinted aviator glasses that he wore in all lighting conditions. He paced in the lobby, rehearsing the speech he would deliver in the middle of the awards ceremony.

Mitchell had been one of the major acting commodities when Hollywood was under the studio system. Movie stars were little more than indentured servants, signed to contracts by the founders of the motion picture industry. Their acting services were loaned out from time to time to competitive studios, but they were the property of the contract holders. Part of the pact for being high-priced chattel was that their indiscretions were kept private by the power of the moviemakers. The police were paid off to cover up their peccadilloes, no matter how minor or felonious. Unplanned pregnancies never happened, and unwanted babies disappeared without the public ever getting wind of them. Infidelities were swept under the red carpet, and the stars' sheen remained untarnished. The studios used publicity to replace the reality of the stars' private lives with the fantasies they created that were more consistent with the on-screen images that the public adored.

Then in the sixties, things seemed to get away from the Hollywood studio heads. Agents gained power when the actors became independent. With that change, the hands-off policy with the media and law enforcement vanished. Arthur often said that it marked the time when the inmates started running the asylum.

Coop had benefited from the new structure where the sky was the limit on salaries. Back-end deals became the norm with big stars, allowing them to participate directly in the gross profits of the pictures.

With the unlimited income potential also came the lack of protection of personal privacy. Someone was always trying to take Coop's photo, find out who was sharing his bed, and most of all, snooping around to discover the nature of the rift that drove him and Sirena apart.

The couple had made a pact never to disclose the intimate details of their marriage. At first when Coop suggested they see an attorney for a prenuptial agreement before they walked down the aisle, Sirena turned to him with tears in her eyes. "I'm not going to sign the terms of my divorce before I've signed our wedding license. That's not how I want to start out in our marriage. I'm sticking with you for life," she said, stroking his thigh.

"I'm in this forever too, but you have to be reasonable about this, babe."

"What's between us is between us, and you've got to trust me to keep our lives private. If you love me enough to marry me, you love me enough to trust me," she pleaded. Her fingers caressed his thick hair, and then she coaxed his mouth with a deep, lingering kiss.

He breathed in her intoxicating scent and put his arms around her waist, drawing her closer. "I do trust you, but I *don't* trust the courts and the easy access to documents. People have the best intentions when they're in love, and I think we'll always be in love, but I need some insurance before I go through with our wedding."

"The only insurance you need is on that sports car you drive too fast and hopefully won't ram it into a brick wall someday," she said. If you think our marriage is going to crash and burn also, then we've both got to give this thing some serious thought."

"I'm sorry you feel that way," he said, standing up and looking down at her.

A tear raced down her cheek. "And I'm sorry that we can't get married full of joy instead of full of doom."

"That's a tad bit dramatic. I love you and I want to marry you," Coop said.

"Well, I never thought I'd sign a prenup, and I'm not so sure I will," she said and stormed out of his house.

Two days later, the pair met in his lawyer's office in a high-rise in Century City. Sirena disguised herself with a long black wig, and Coop dressed in oversized jogging clothes with a baseball cap pulled over his eyes. Once inside, they looked at each other and laughed at their getups.

The secretary said, "Mr. Stein will see you now."

They walked down a long corridor lined with original oil paintings. Coop looked at misty street scenes of Paris with horseless carriages on wide boulevards. Outside Marvin Stein's office, a Brâncuși bronze statue sat in a lit niche. Inside, a swirling, brooding postimpressionist painting was perched above Marvin's desk.

"Must have been a lot of broken homes to pay for this art gallery," Sirena said.

"No, just plenty of satisfied clients," Marvin replied, motioning for them to take a seat on his couch. His secretary lingered at the door, staring at Coop.

"Lisa, why don't you get them something to drink? What do you two want?"

"Anything diet," Sirena said.

"Anything alcoholic," Coop said and rubbed her knee.

"Sirena, I want you to feel completely comfortable here. No one is against you, and this will ultimately be for both your and Coop's peace of mind and will take the worry out of what might happen in the future," Marvin said.

"I'm here but don't patronize me," Sirena said, twirling a lock of her silvery hair.

"I promise you will be well taken care of—no matter what happens in life. I just want to make sure that what goes on in this marriage stays in this marriage," Coop said.

"Okay, let's hear what the two of you cooked up," Sirena said. "You know, I'm going to make a lot of money while we're married, so I might want some protection from him in case his popularity starts to slide."

Marvin looked only at Coop while he spoke. "We'll go through these documents slowly and carefully to make sure that the two of you understand them fully and that they are written to your specifications."

Marvin ran through the eventual division of property that was currently owned or would be purchased. He put a number on the percentage of cars to which Sirena would be entitled. Monies that were accrued after their marriage would be considered community property, if not commingled to maintain enterprises or properties that belonged to either party before their union. The list went on ad infinitum about the number and category of worldly goods that could be divided. At the end of the property discussion, Marvin pulled out a separate folder from the portfolio case. He pressed the intercom button and told his secretary to hold all calls.

He removed his half-glasses from his nose. Marvin opened the packet of documents and handed a set of copies to each of them. "This is a caveat stipulating that if certain terms of the enclosed privacy clauses are violated, then Sirena forfeits the generous financial settlement you have specified. The one-hundred-million split is null and void, and then she is only eligible to receive one primary residence, two cars totaling up to $200,000, and child support, in the event there are minor dependents."

"Whoa, that's a hefty penalty for loose lips," Sirena said and puckered for a kiss from Coop.

"Furthermore, it prohibits any private or public discussion of Coop's medical conditions or the details of your sexual activities with each other before and after marriage."

"And what about me? Can he run around town saying I'm a lousy lay or something like that if he decides to run off with his next leading lady?" Sirena's alabaster skin turned crimson.

"No, we'll both agree that our sex life and physical conditions are off-limits for discussion," Coop said.

"So what do I get if he's vindictive and spreads a lot of lies about me?"

"First of all, this is all moot because we're not going to get divorced—ever!" Coop gently pulled her chin in his direction to look into her eyes.

"Then why the hell are we going through this exercise?" Sirena pushed the papers away from her.

"With prior earnings as substantial as in this case, it's really standard procedure," Marvin said. "Some of this contract is boilerplate, fill-in-the-blank kind of stuff. The privacy issues and exact financial sums are, of course, tailored to your specific needs. I'm going to step out of the room for a few minutes and give the two of you a chance to talk this over." Marvin walked over from his desk to squeeze each of their shoulders before he left the room. "Let Lisa know if you need anything."

The two stars remained on the couch, each staring forward.

"Yeah, I need to think it over if I really want to go through with this marriage," Sirena said with a deep sigh.

"Oh, that makes me feel confident that you really love me for myself and not for my money."

"Go straight to hell!" Sirena slammed the papers on the coffee table and started to walk toward the door, but Coop grabbed her hand. A current of attraction ran through his fingers.

Tears escaped down his face, softening his features. "Sirena, don't leave me. If this is the deal-breaker in our marriage, then forget it."

"Forget the marriage?" she asked, searching his dampened blue eyes.

"No, forget about the prenup. If I trust you enough to marry you, I trust you completely."

She kissed the tears from his cheeks and then wrapped her arms around him. She whispered softly like a mother soothing an errant child, "I'll never let you down. We're not going to part, and you know that I will always do the right thing and never betray you. I promise." They kissed passionately and clung to each other.

After a soft knock on the door, Marvin reentered his office. "I should say that it looks like you two have reached some kind of agreement. Now let's get back to business. Who wants to sign first?"

"Marvin, we're going to skip the prenuptial agreement," Coop said.

"Whose idea was this, might I ask?"

"It was both of ours," Sirena answered with a butter-melting smile.

"Well then, all that's left to do is to wish you *mazel tov* and to dance at your wedding. But before you leave, let Lisa get your signatures on a document that says you've agreed not to sign the prenup. Sit tight. She'll be just a minute. Good luck, you crazy kids."

Marvin muttered under his breath as he left his office, "Madness! *Oy*, such *meshugas!*"

18
FRANCINE &
ARTHUR

For years, Francine had enjoyed an intimate working relationship with Coop, her favorite star. Being with him at the Movie Constellation Awards ceremony was the icing on the cake for the special attention she had given him, her biggest A-list client.

She had groomed him and had protected his image in the press. It was a difficult balancing act to keep his name in front of the public without reaching a level of oversaturation. Coop religiously guarded his image and rarely accepted television shows or magazine interviews. If he was ever in print, it was on the condition that the article would be the featured story and his photo would appear on the cover. While he was on top, there would never be a piece about Preston Cooper buried in the back of a magazine next to a recipe for artichoke dip and tests to determine if your child was gifted. Francine controlled access to Coop. Even the studio executives had to get her permission. He was "her boy."

Coop pressed his veto power to the limit when approving photographs. By contract, he was allowed a fifty percent kill right on his likeness to be used in any publicity materials, including one-sheet posters, billboards, and print ads. He was hands-on regarding the selection of the key art for his films.

After the photo shoot by world-famous Elaine Richter for *Big House*, he mulled through the stack of prints, tossing most of them aside. Even though a mock-up session had been held, where stand-ins had posed in the completed set and costumes before Coop and Sirena breezed in for the actual shot, he rejected image after image.

Coop finally allowed for the ones with him and Sirena to be used because the stars would not sit together beyond their split. Sirena had approved her individual poses, but Coop was exercising his control to have his solo shots repeated.

Although it cost the studio double the top photographer's rate, another session was arranged. "Who the hell does Coop think he is? Get Francine on the horn and read her the riot act. I'd better see some magic marker checkmarks next to the revised round of photos," Arthur ranted, throwing the stack of glossy eight by tens on his desk. "These shots are drop-dead gorgeous, and not one of them is worth rejecting."

Charlie retreated to her office. Passing Gabe's desk, she said, "Get Tsarina Francina on the phone for me."

Gabe patched her through to Francine. "Hi, girlfriend. I guess you heard about the photo shoot. Elaine agreed to another date, but she's not a happy camper. I don't think anyone except Queen Elizabeth has given her such a hard time."

"Well, we're dealing with the 'King of Hollywood,' so she'd better get used to it. Coop thought his ears looked out of proportion, and he wasn't happy with his teeth in any of the shots," Francine said.

"The product tie-in deal I arranged is going to be lost if we don't go into production with the marketing materials. This is the last chance, photo kill rights or not. I suggest we get better approvals on the next shoot," Charlie insisted.

"If they're good enough, you will. If not, you won't. Gotta run." There was a sharp click.

"That bitch!" Charlie shouted, loud enough for Gabe to hear. She marched into Arthur's office, pausing as he waved to her that he was on the phone.

"Yes, Francine ... We'll make sure Coop looks good. And if we don't get it this time, Elaine will just have to suck it up and shoot it again," Arthur purred.

Charlie couldn't believe she had been caught again by Arthur's "good cop-bad cop" routine.

A few weeks later, the second batch of photos arrived to the marketing department, equally as splendid as the first. Francine sent her associate, Mercedes Le Blanc, to deliver them to Coop for his approval. Coop also took a good look at the lithe brunette with a hint of a French accent who helped him sift through the stacks of photos. He had briefly met her before in Paris, but she looked different to him in the new light of his being single.

To everyone's relief, several images were selected and were immediately dropped into the one-sheet layouts that were overdue at the printers. The meeting with Coop and Mercedes was considered a success by all.

19
COOP &
MERCEDES

Aᴼᴛᴇʀ ᴛʜᴀᴛ ꜰɪʀꜱᴛ ᴍᴇᴇᴛɪɴɢ, Coop had been requesting that Mercedes Le Blanc assist Francine when she needed support from her staff. The three of them were scheduled to travel abroad during the first week in September.

Big House, Little Lady was an official entry in the Normandy Film Festival held a month after the movie had opened in the United States. An entourage from Silverlake Pictures arrived in an elegant seaside town in northwestern France. Arthur, Teeni, Charlie, Francine, Mercedes, and the cast traveled on the same plane, but Sirena's flight was delayed.

The filmmakers were there to introduce American films to the European movie distributors. The studio was committed to presenting *Big House* as more than cinema—positioning it as an event that captured part of American history.

Chauffeured from the airport, Francine and Mercedes went over some of the plans for the weeklong event. Francine decided she would leave right after the screening and press conferences, and Mercedes would stay to finish up some of the details.

They talked, shuffling through papers, as they drove past the lush countryside dotted with grazing black-and-white cattle. Periodically the driver interrupted them to point out historic sites. His speech was a thick cassoulet of French and English, difficult for Francine to understand. "*Zee* English let many of these lovely *fermes*, ah … farmhouses, while on holiday. It feels like home to *zem*. Regard *zee* architecture with cream façades decorated with brown beams."

"Just like English Tudor houses," Francine said.

"Madam, that's because Duke *Guillaume de Normandie*, William the Conqueror, as you call him, brought this style to Britain after he won the British Isles in 1066. While you are here, you must try our Camembert and drink calvados—uh, *zee* brandy from apples."

"Very interesting, but could you put the travelogue on hold? We've got to go over a few things before we get to the hotel," Francine snapped.

The driver snorted like a bull and adjusted his cap. "*Les touristes américains sont détestés!*" he muttered under his breath.

"*Faites attention à votre compartement.*" Mercedes reprimanded him to mind his manners.

"*Oui mademoiselle.*" The driver remained silent until he pulled into the driveway of the picturesque hotel. The weathered, shingled rooftop sat like a pointed nightcap on an elegant empress. Window boxes burst with red geraniums skirting the balconies that accented the sprawling exterior with green timber lattice, checkered stone cornices, and turrets. One side of the hotel faced the charming storybook town, and the other overlooked the English Channel lined by powdery white beaches and a curving boardwalk. Nestled between the classic architecture, the casino commanded attention with its white sensuous curves, a bastion of the elegance and refinement of the Belle Époque.

Francine stepped into the hotel lobby and was ushered to one of the richly patterned, overstuffed chairs. The sunlight filtered through the windows, casting a golden glow on the ornately carved wooden panels.

"Hard to believe anyone could conduct business in such a gorgeous place. I feel like I'm some elegant Victorian lady off for a grand seaside holiday away from the hustle bustle of gay Paris," Mercedes said, using the French pronunciation for the city of lights, *Par-ee.*"

"You're beginning to sound like a tourist from Iowa who's never left the U.S. This festival is one of my favorite spots—not quite as high profile as Cannes. Go see if you can speed things up around here. We've got work to do."

Mercedes spoke in her native tongue to the front desk clerk.

Within a matter of minutes, the bell captain greeted Francine. She pointed to her designer luggage, a small valise and a tote, which were whisked onto his trolley. "I'll go with the bags to my room. Yours is next to mine but around the corner. Mercedes, do me a favor. Stop in the sundries shop and pick up something for my upset stomach. I must have overdone the pâté in the airport VIP lounge while we were waiting for customs. Just knock on my door."

Mercedes walked through the lobby and lingered at a display window full of diamond watches, some of which were worth more than her annual salary. They were temptations for impulse buyers who won at the nearby casino. She entered the small sundries shop and browsed through French and American magazines before looking for the bottle of medicine for Francine.

Outside the shop, Mercedes heard a ruckus—people shouting and shuffling around. She put down the fashion magazine and peeked out to determine the cause of the commotion. The staid atmosphere of the hotel lobby erupted into a frenzy. About a dozen people engulfed Preston Cooper. Jamaal Kenter from the studio's security team implored the fans to disperse, but to no avail.

Mercedes rushed into the lobby. *"Laissez les gens respirer!"* She reproached the crowd in a voice that cut through the chaos.

The people started to retreat to give Coop some air, clearing a path for Jamaal to jostle his way next to the star.

"Mercedes to the rescue," Coop said.

"I try my best. I told everyone to back off."

"Where's your boss lady?"

"She's upstairs, not feeling very well. I've got to bring her something to calm her stomach. Do you still need my help?"

"Let's see—since the festival doesn't get warmed up until tomorrow, why don't you grab a bite with me tonight."

"I'll check with Francine and find out what she's got on tap for me."

"Don't worry. I'll give her a call and tell her. Can you be ready soon because I want to take a look around the town while it's still light? I don't ever get a few free minutes before all hell breaks loose."

"Okay, I'm in room 200," Mercedes said.

"I'm in the Presidential Suite."

"Yes, I know. I booked it for you. Give me a call when you're ready. I've got to deliver some medicine to her right away. Poor Francine looked about the same shade of green as the wall trim around here."

A few minutes later, Mercedes knocked on Francine's door.

"Come in. It's not locked," Francine croaked.

Mercedes entered and saw Francine lying on the bed. She lay propped on a mountain of decorative pillows, with the phone against her ear. "Coop, I'm really okay, sweetheart. Nice of you to call." She grabbed the wastebasket. "Really, I could join the two of you for dinner if you'd like. We could go over the press conference and some of the scheduling."

Francine motioned for Mercedes to open the bottle of stomach medicine. She balanced the phone against a pillow. "No, I don't think I'm contagious. If you think I shouldn't... Okay, I'll check in with you later," Francine said. She hung up.

"Mercedes, I guess you can babysit him this afternoon. Just keep Coop out of the press until tomorrow, and try to stay clear of Sirena when she lands. Loose lips sink flicks. Check with Charlie and find out Sirena's schedule. I don't think she's arriving until tomorrow but double-check."

"No problem." Mercedes glanced at her watch.

"Take Jamaal with you. We don't need another incident where Coop is mobbed," Francine said.

"How did you know?"

"Sweetheart, these ears hear about everything!" Francine slipped off her earrings and tossed them on the night table.

"Will do. I'll call Jamaal in a second."

"I feel like crap. Since I last saw you, I puked my guts out four times," she said, hugging the trash basket.

"Did you call the hotel doctor?"

"He's on his way up."

There was a knock, and Mercedes welcomed the doctor into the hotel room. She opened the balcony doors to let the refreshing sea breeze fill the room that reeked of illness. Mercedes gazed at the white beach dotted with a rainbow of umbrellas. The sea glistened in the sunlight like a Monet painting.

"I'll get settled next door. Let me know if you need anything."

Mercedes went to her room and opened the curtains to reveal the hotel's parking lot. She hoped one day she'd rate an ocean view.

A few minutes later, Francine rang Mercedes's room. "I must have picked up some kind of bug on that damn airplane. First class or not, I'm sick as a dog."

"Sorry, Francine. Is there anything I can do?"

"No, the doctor gave me some disgusting-tasting prescription elixir, and I feel like the room's spinning."

"Just take it easy, and let's hope it will pass by the morning."

"Check with Charlie and find out if everything is good to go tomorrow at the press conference in the garden." Francine's voice trailed off.

"Will do. Rest well." Mercedes hung up, and then the phone instantly rang again.

"Are you ready?"

"Sorry?" Mercedes said.

"It's Coop. Let's get out of here for a while. I've got a car behind the hotel. Let's go."

"Okay, give me a few minutes." Mercedes surveyed herself in the mirror, frowning at her business suit. She dumped her suitcase on the bed and plowed through her clothes until she found a pink low-cut top she usually wore under a jacket. She slipped on a pair of tight jeans and dashed out the door, headed toward the elevators, then doubled back to put out the Do Not Disturb sign.

When Mercedes arrived at the lobby, she was thankful it was clear of anyone she knew. She skirted around the sedate furniture and potted palms, finding her way to the back courtyard. In the cobbled driveway, Coop waved to her from a gleaming silver Ferrari convertible.

"How'd you get this car so fast?" she asked.

"I've got my ways," he said with a Slavic accent like in old spy movies.

"So much for being inconspicuous."

"Hey, this is France. They're used to seeing racy cars and the jet set. I've got somewhere in mind that's a little different."

"Francine might need me."

"Don't worry. I'll take care of *Madam Sweetheart*," he said, laughing.

Coop gunned the engine. Running like a linebacker from around the stone corner of the building, Jamaal shouted, "Hey, wait up!"

Coop peeled out of the driveway onto the main road. He said to Mercedes, "Where we're going, we don't need any chaperones."

The sun, perched high in the sky, illuminated the area like a scene in a fairy tale. They passed the casino with a huge banner of Coop and Sirena in a steamy embrace from *Big House, Little Lady* draping the rotunda. They sped through the town and then hit the open road. Castles and orchards whizzed by in a pastel blur. Coop motored down the lane along an estuary of the River Touques and crossed a bridge.

"This leads to Trouville-sur-Mer, a laid-back town away from the fast pace of the film festival," he said.

"It looks lovely. I've been to this area before, but for some reason I never made it over to Trouville."

"Look, let's come back here tonight for dinner. I know a quaint little bistro along the waterside. I've got a better idea for now. You game?" Coop asked.

"*Mai oui*," she said, feeling a twinge of excitement.

"I don't know if you're up for it, but I'd like to see the landing beaches on Normandy. It might be a bit tough to handle."

"My *grand-père* fought in the resistance when he was young. My father took our family to Normandy to see where he had fought, but I was little and don't remember it well. We came to the States when I was five," Mercedes said.

The Ferrari ate up the road. It handled the hairpin turns with ease and stopped in a heartbeat when they had to break for a flock of goats that wandered into the country lane.

Coop parked the car on a narrow street in the tiny seaside village of Arromanches. He and Mercedes teetered down the steep, cobbled lanes, holding on to each other to maintain their balance.

"Can't you almost hear the fighting, see the soldiers darting from building to building?" Coop said, looking at the stone structures surrounding them.

"It just seems like a sleepy little town to me. Look at that beautiful window box overflowing with geraniums. Only the satellite dishes on the rooftops remind me that we're in the twenty-first century."

They reached the bottom of the hill and faced the calm, blue expanse.

"What are those concrete things in the water?" Mercedes asked.

"Barges that turned the tide of the war. The Allies set up those concrete barriers for the landings, to make a sheltered harbor. They towed them from England across the Channel to make an artificial bay. If it had been a full moon, they wouldn't have been able to pull off the element of surprise."

"You can't get away with anything these days. With infrared video cameras tracking our troops' every move, everyone watched the start of the Gulf War on television. Reporters were even tracking the number of pizza delivery trucks at the Pentagon to figure out how close we were to the invasion, and everyone knew when the first bullet was fired. Hey, but you're used to invasive press by now, I guess," Mercedes said.

"I'll never get used to it, but it comes with the territory of being famous. I wouldn't be surprised if some asshole paparazzo jumped out of that bunker below."

Coop and Mercedes climbed down a sandy embankment onto the grassy hillside to get a better look at a small stone mound carved out of the hill.

"Look at this pillbox. The Germans sat in here and picked off our guys as they landed," Coop said. "I've played a soldier several times but have never actually been one. Can't imagine the kind of courage it takes to jump out of a landing ship directly into the face of oncoming enemy fire."

"It makes it all so real, seeing this stretch of beach and imagining how many people died in this little plot of land," Mercedes said. She wiped a tear with the back of her hand.

Coop nestled closer, putting his arm around her. He felt her body fit naturally next to his. They climbed to the top of the hill and gazed down at the sunlight dancing on the water. Mercedes wondered if they were going to kiss, but instead, Coop brushed a windswept lock of hair out of her eyes and then led her back toward the car.

"Let's keep going," he said. The engine purred. "We've got another stop—the Normandy American Cemetery and Memorial. You can't come to the landing beaches and leave without seeing it."

He drove into the gated lot of the monument on a plateau above Omaha Beach and the English Channel. Coop and Mercedes emerged from the car, met by a cool breeze. They followed the path to the entrance of the immense cemetery. As far as the eye could see, rows of white crosses, interrupted by occasional Stars of David, filled the landscape to the horizon. Almost ten thousand American soldiers were laid to rest in the perfectly manicured graveyard.

Coop and Mercedes didn't speak, silenced by their surroundings. With their two hands tightly entwined, they moved down the first row, pausing to read the headstones, and then headed for the memorial. Coop crouched on the marble steps, his head in his hands. Mercedes sank down quietly next to him. Together they prayed for the countless dead who were laid to rest before them.

The sun lowered in the sky, and the flags on the monument flapped in the light gusts. Coop stood and reached for Mercedes's hand, feeling a combination of comfort and excitement at her touch. They walked silently back to the sleek car parked outside the cemetery gates.

Coop gunned the engine, sputtering gravel as he maneuvered the car onto the narrow road. The wide tires hugged the curves as they drove through town and headed for the open spaces.

Mercedes flicked away a tear. "I could just imagine the carnage." She leaned over and kissed Coop's cheek.

He turned his head slightly so their lips met and then flipped his eyes back to the road to keep from crashing into an old cart full of hay. "Let's grab something to eat. You can't get a bad meal in France."

"That's what my parents always say," Mercedes agreed. "Dad hates to eat out because he says Mama's cooking is the only good food he's had since he moved to the States."

"So are you handy around the kitchen?" Coop asked.

"I think I'm better in another room of the house."

"Does that apply to hotel rooms too?"

"We'll see." Her eyes sparkled.

As they drove into the port of Trouville, fishermen on the shore were gathering their nets in an age-old rhythm. The setting sun painted a golden cast on the beach and the surrounding buildings. They passed the casino and traveled along the road that skirted the coast. Coop pulled into a driveway behind a quaint white house with dark green shutters.

"Hope you like this place. It's got the best bouillabaisse I've ever had."

"What does a guy from the middle of Texas know about good fish?" she kidded.

"Right. I grew up on frozen fish sticks. Trust me though, it's great—and very private."

The hostess smiled with a hint of recognition when she saw Coop enter the restaurant.

"*Une table pour deux*," Mercedes said.

"I have a nice one in the corner," she answered in heavily accented English, never taking her eyes off Coop.

"*Très bien*," Mercedes replied with a note of irritation in her voice. She wondered if the woman had detected a slight Americanization in her pronunciation, not realizing the reply was meant for the American movie star, not for her.

Soft evening light filtered through the lace curtains that dotted the room. The couple sat side by side at a corner table near the fireplace filled with a profusion of dried lavender and sunflowers since it was too early in the season for a fire. Coop looked into Mercedes's dark brown eyes that shone with excitement. Just as they leaned toward each other to kiss, the waiter inquired what they would like to drink.

"Timing is everything," Coop said. He laughed, shaking his head, and then ordered a bottle of the most expensive champagne on the menu.

"That's a rare treat," Mercedes said in approval.

"A special occasion calls for a little extra celebration."

"Yes, being the featured movie at the Normandy Film Festival is extremely special," she said.

"That's not the special moment I'm talking about."

The waiter carefully poured, tilting the flutes to control the flow of the bubbling liquid. Coop and Mercedes intertwined their arms and drank from each other's glasses, as they had seen in countless Hollywood romantic movies.

They took a sip and moved toward each other for the kiss that had been interrupted. Laced with fine champagne, Coop's lips tasted cool and delicious. Mercedes felt light-headed from the way his tongue explored her mouth, seeking places that made her whole body tingle.

She had figured he'd be a good kisser from watching his on-screen love scenes, and he surpassed her fantasy. She wanted more.

They ordered their meals and then stared at each other as if they had discovered a rare treasure. The waiter quietly delivered a basket of brioche and a bowl of country pâté as airy as whipped cream.

Eating no longer appealed to Mercedes. Fearful that her stomach might swell, she nibbled on a few crumbs of warm bread.

"It's been so long since I've been on a date without having a camera shoved in my face," Coop said.

"Is that what this is, a date? I thought we were working together and this is just part of business."

"I don't know about you, but I don't usually stick my tongue down my business associate's throat," Coop said, sounding like a rejected schoolboy.

"And I don't get so hot that I'm going to slide off my seat for any of our other clients," she said laughing, trying to recapture the mood.

"That sounds very promising." He pulled her close for a long, hungry kiss.

At an adjacent table, a husband and wife turned their children's heads toward their own plates. The woman muttered in disgust, *"Ces Américains!"*

Mercedes and Coop inched closer together. She whispered, "I guess Trouville is more provincial than Paris."

Coop hoisted his glass and toasted, *"Vive l'amour!"*

The waiter delivered two bowls of bouillabaisse to the table. Clam shells, pieces of lobster, and hunks of white flaky fish floated in a fragrant broth. Coop and Mercedes each took a spoonful, locked eyes, and in unison dropped their spoons and kissed over the steaming soup.

Coop signaled for the waiter. *"L'addition, s'il vous plaît,"* he said with a slight Texan twang.

The server grimaced at the uneaten bowls of bouillabaisse and seemed doubly offended by Coop's mangled French accent. He turned on his heels to get the check.

"Now you're really impressing me," Mercedes said.

The bill arrived, and Coop pulled out a credit card.

When the waiter returned with the slip, Mercedes warned Coop, "Usually service is included in this country."

Coop scribbled a large number on the line above the total. "I'm a big tipper."

Mercedes knew that the dinner with the four-hundred-dollar bottle of champagne would end up on Coop's expense report to be paid for by the studio.

"I like a man who's not afraid to give," she said.

The pair got up and passed by the family busily enjoying their crème brûlées. The father winked at Coop, while the mother diverted her attention from her dessert to scowl at Mercedes like she belonged in a French whorehouse.

As Coop headed for the door, a lone man entered the restaurant. Recognizing his broad frame in the dim light, Coop approached him. "How the hell did you find us?" he asked.

It didn't take much doing," Jamaal replied. "The Ferrari you rented has a tracking device. How were the landing beaches? I figured you were pretty safe by yourselves in the countryside."

"This is a little too much like big brother is watching me."

"Look, you could be a target for kidnapping or could easily be mobbed," Jamaal said. "Remember that time you were at a movie theme park in Orlando and a crowd of tourists almost ripped the shirt off your back to literally get a piece of you? Man, I'm just trying to do my job—to keep you safe."

"I guess he's got a point," Mercedes said, joining the two men.

"And let me tell you this, Mercedes; if something were to happen to you and Coop, you probably wouldn't even rate having your name spelled out in the news."

"That's a bit rough. Look, thanks for the help, but we're fine. Take the rest of the night off, Jamaal," Coop said.

"It's your ball game. Just give me an idea where you'll be," Jamaal said.

"From here, we're going back to the hotel. I don't want to be disturbed for the rest of the evening, and I don't want to be followed into the hotel. Got that?"

"Loud and clear. Here's my cell phone number if you have any problems. You two, have a good evening."

The three of them walked outside to the gravel parking lot. "You don't mind if I watch you get into your car, do you?" Jamaal asked. "Occupational habit."

"Be my guest. Knock yourself out. Thanks, man." Coop opened the door for Mercedes and then scurried around to the driver's side. He sped onto the dark country road.

"That boy's going to be the death of me, or himself, by the way he drives," Jamaal muttered as he watched the red taillights disappear around the curve.

Coop's eyes were glued to the road as he accelerated with each turn. Mercedes's hand rested on his knee.

"Sometimes I get sick and tired of people watching my every move. I can't even take a leak without it appearing on the pages of some tabloid that I was caught holding my own dick in public."

"What if someone else was holding it in private?" she joked with a lilting laugh.

"Now *that* sounds interesting," he said.

"Well, it can be easily arranged." Her hand moved up his thigh to the bulge in his pants.

"If you keep that up, we're going to end up like Princess Grace plunging down a deep ravine, but they'll find me at the bottom with my big famous smile plastered across my face."

"Please just stay alive, and I'll hold the thought of making you smile," she said.

While they drove to the hotel, they devised a plan to meet in his suite. Mercedes was afraid that Francine might hear them in the adjoining room.

Coop dropped off Mercedes at the casino next door. She felt conspicuous in her casual clothes because formal attire was required at the tables in the posh gaming rooms. She passed by glamorous people in long gowns and tuxedos as she hurried to the beach side exit. Her pulse quickened as she followed the boardwalk connecting the casino to the hotel. The moon shone brightly over the water, and the hotel glowed like an enchanted castle. Mercedes had to laugh at herself for thinking that a real Prince Charming, with a hard-on, would be waiting for her upstairs.

Coop entered the lobby devoid of guests who were either at late dinners or at film screenings. At the front desk, he requested the key to his suite, wishing the grand old hotel had converted to plastic key cards instead of maintaining ornate brass ones. Usually Jamaal secured the key and preceded him to open the door and inspect the premises. Tonight Coop told the desk clerk he would go alone.

He rode the elevator to the top floor and walked to the corner suite with its own private entrance flanked by a pair of porcelain urns filled with sprays of orchids. He entered the room and dashed into one of the three bathrooms to freshen up before Mercedes arrived, stashing his box of syringes in a drawer. Coop felt as excited as a schoolboy on a first date. Unlike when he was a teen, he felt fairly certain he was going to get lucky.

He pulled back the satin bedspread, and then he turned on a lamp in the living room. Coop kept the bedroom lights off and figured the single bulb would provide just the right atmosphere. He tried out a variety of settings—the bed, the chair—and finally settled on the couch. On second thought, Coop turned off the lamp in the sitting room and flipped on the powder room overhead for backlight. He poured two glasses of chilled champagne the studio had sent as a welcome gift and placed them on the coffee table.

In the meantime, Mercedes entered the hotel lobby from the beach entrance and took the elevator up to her room on the opposite side of the building from Coop's suite. She darted into her room and quickly brushed her teeth. She rummaged through her closet, letting clothes fly until she found what she was looking for. Gently closing the door, she made sure the Do Not Disturb sign was displayed on the knob.

Mercedes climbed the service stairs up to the fourth-floor penthouse. The door from the stairwell was unlocked. She tiptoed so her sandals wouldn't make flopping sounds as she walked down the hall. She reached the entrance to Coop's suit and pushed the door that had been left ajar.

Mercedes crept into the dimly lit room. The moonlight streamed in from the doors that opened onto a wrought iron balcony, casting swirling patterns on the walls. She spotted Coop's gleaming body on the couch, invitingly erect. She could hear his soft breathing over her racing heartbeat. Covered in a white terry robe, she slowly approached him. Without a word, she let the wrap drop to the floor. A silvery ray of light bathed her naked figure.

"You sure know how to dress for an occasion," Coop said. He took her hand and pulled her down toward him. Coop and Mercedes kissed deeply, and then she nestled her face in his neck and started working her way down his well-muscled body.

His hands moved over her taught belly and then sought her silky warmth.

"How are you going to get out of here wearing a bathrobe?" he asked between kisses.

"I stuffed my bikini in the pocket. I'll just say I was going to the beach for a late or early swim, depending on when I leave."

He glanced at the flutes of champagne and said, "Mind if I take a dip now?"

She picked up the glass and took a sip. Then she moved it toward his body. "Let's see if the bubbles really do tickle."

Coop couldn't believe his good fortune in finding a girl who was game for anything. He wondered if it was because she was French, and he wanted to find out what else she had in store for him.

"Let's move to the bed. We'll take the champagne with us," Mercedes said.

She got up, swirling from arousal, and waited for him to hold her. He scooped her up and carried her into the bedroom. At that moment, the Normandy Film Festival and Francine seemed very far away.

20
COOP &
SIRENA

T HE ORCHESTRA PLAYED A FANFARE to announce the commence-
ment of the Movie Constellation Awards ceremony. Francine
clasped Coop's hand and said, "This is your night, sweetheart. You've
already won a Silver Orb and a Film Performers Award. This movie's
going to out win *Titanic*."

The music swelled as the cameras panned the star-studded audience. The eighteen-foot monitors on the sides of the stage magnified
the live action for those, like Charlie and Gabe, sitting in the less
desirable seats. Coop smiled broadly into the camera, his comely
face filling the screen. At his side, Francine was cropped out of the
tight frame. The screen reverted to the Constance Award logo as the
telecast cut to a commercial.

"Mercedes should have been here," Coop said.

"I had to send her to London to do some advance work for the
Royal Premiere. She'll be back next week."

"She worked so hard on this picture, right along with you,"
Coop said.

"Mercedes is just too valuable, and I needed her eye for detail. I didn't realize it was so important to you that she attend tonight."

"She should have been rewarded with a ticket. I'll do something special when she gets back."

"Great. I'm sure she'll appreciate anything you send her."

"I mean that I'll personally make it up to her," Coop said.

"I guess you're just stuck with her dreary old boss tonight."

Francine was pleased that Mercedes was abroad and wouldn't be part of the evening's festivities. Francine would accompany Coop to the official Constellation Ball directly after the show and then to a series of after-parties hosted by the various media. Most importantly, she would be nearby in the press conference at the end of the telecast in case Coop needed moral support and would make sure that he said the right thing. She was positive he would walk away with the top acting honor. There was a strong chance that Sirena would do the same, as *Big House, Little Lady* was the odds-on favorite to make a clean sweep of the Movie Constellation Awards.

Coop and Sirena had only been seen together in the same room recently when they were at other film industry events. They sat at opposite ends of the aisle at the theater, eliminating a chance to photograph them near each other.

When the camera panned to Sirena during the ceremony, she snuggled close to Ethan Dean Traynor, whispering in his ear.

The show's host, Willy Rivers, performed a comedic medley featuring the five nominated Best Pictures. When he spoofed *Big House, Little Lady*, Coop flashed a broad smile and waved at the camera. His expression didn't reveal he was thinking about how he had gone into the filming of the movie almost a year and a half ago with high hopes for his future with his wife, Sirena.

Sharon Roundtree from the *Movie Times Journal* had interviewed the pair for a profile shortly before they wrapped shooting *Big House*. She had been granted access for one hour in the couple's rented home on location.

Sharon had asked, "Now that the two of you are a married couple and are acting together, is this the start of a trend? Do you envision yourselves as the next Bogie and Bacall?"

"I'd prefer to think of us more like Paul Newman and Joanne Woodward," Coop said, laughing. "They made ten movies together, over double the classic film couple's output."

"Filmmaking is something that we want to share in life. These movies are going to be our babies, our legacy we can look back on." Sirena snuggled next to Coop.

"Does this mean that there aren't going to be any little Coops and Sirenas in the future?" the reporter asked with a tinge of sadness.

"No, it just means that our films are our professional offspring; acting is only a job, but it's the best job in the world," Coop said.

"We want lots of children. But not just right now," Sirena added.

"So you two are trying to have kids?"

"My motto is practice makes perfect, and we'll keep 'doing it' until we get it right," Coop said with twinkle in his eye.

"Now that you brought up the subject yourself, any truth to the rumors about the torrid sex scenes in *Big House, Little Lady*?" the interviewer probed.

"What rumors?" Coop asked coyly.

"About the two of you being naughty on camera. We heard it was a closed set on the love scenes."

"Let's just say that you'll have to see the finished film, and hopefully, we'll have done our job of bringing Jack London's philosophy of life and love to contemporary moviegoers," Coop replied in an announcer's voice.

"Oh, so now you're telling me it's a message film?"

"God no, the producers would kill me!" He laughed and shifted in his chair. "Messages don't usually attract audiences. This is a timeless story, a period piece that is as relevant and shocking today as it was when it was written decades ago. Most of us have temptations that we struggle to deal with in an ethical way."

"And my character, Paula Forrest, is an early feminist," Sirena added. "She tries to remain free of conventions of the era that restrict women in what they wear and what they can think and say. This role let me stretch, showing a side of me that hasn't been explored before."

"From what we hear, we see quite a lot of a side of you that's never been filmed. What was it like to shoot the scenes when you were completely nude? We heard there's a glimpse of Coop's backside, but you're in a wet garment that reveals all for several scenes in the picture, and then there's about three seconds of you in the buff."

"Those costumes were really amazing and very unforgiving," Sirena said. "I had to work out with my personal trainer for about three months to make sure there weren't any ripples or bulges that didn't belong. I had to straddle a horse while I plunged into a pond with almost nothing on so often for loads of takes that I started getting used to it. There was a little bit of chafing, I admit!" She giggled and crossed her legs.

"Do you mean you're into 'going commando' now?" Sharon asked as she took notes.

"Let's just say that the wardrobe was very liberating. I did have a simply gorgeous evening gown that I wore at dinner, and thankfully I wasn't trussed with corset stays."

"I'm sure that flimsy bathing suit from the scene with the horse would fetch a pretty penny at auction online. And how was it when you had to be nude, Sirena?"

"I knew I needed to be in shape for those costumes, but the nude scene would have demanded physical perfection. Some of the time there was a body double for the close-ups. There's only so long that I want a camera aimed at my privates." She put her hands in her lap.

"You really do look amazing. I can't imagine where you're hiding a flaw, if you have one," Sharon said.

"This interview is way more fun than I expected," Sirena said.

The reporter turned to Coop and asked more questions about portraying the sexy, adventurous visitor to the ranch, one of the two main male roles in the movie.

"My character, Evan Graham, has to overshadow the lord of the manor, his longtime friend Dick Forrest. Graham tries to win the love of Dick's wife, Paula, who enchanted just about every man who lays eyes on her. I can't tell you how this love triangle ends. No spoilers in this interview." When they were wrapping up the session, Coop asked, "Sharon, this is a cover story, right?"

"Yes. Francine made it clear that neither of you would give an interview unless you're guaranteed the cover."

"Only newcomers and people on the way down land on the inside pages," Coop said.

"No worry there. I'd say you're still firmly planted on the top of the heap. I mean the mountain," Sharon said.

Coop and Sirena had viewed the opportunity to work together on a feature film as a chance to solidify their relationship. Heavy shooting schedules in the past had made their time together as sporadic as summer rainfall in Los Angeles. They both traveled the globe to be on the sets of each other's movies as much as possible, but there were times when they had competing commitments and were apart for several weeks at a stretch.

During those breaks, they shortened the distance with a barrage of phone calls. Some directors objected greatly to the incessant ringtones interrupting the shoots. Coop never kept Sirena waiting on the line and made it crystal clear that it was of utmost importance for him to communicate with his wife, no matter the cost to production.

Sometimes Coop chartered a private jet to visit Sirena on location, and at other times he caught a ride on the studio's Learjet. His last director preferred when Sirena wasn't around because it meant there was a chance he could stick to the production timetable. When Sirena was near the set, the couple would hug and smooch between takes, and then he would have to align the shot when Coop returned to his mark.

Coop, much more the professional, was respectful of Sirena's workday and showed up usually when they were about to wrap.

He never missed a workout on his private gym equipment that was shipped to whatever hotel he was staying in, and if he was going back and forth, the room remained available for his use.

When they accepted the offer to do the movie, Coop and Sirena were excited about being forced to be in the same place over a long period of time. Instead of using a hotel in the Sacramento Valley where the film was on location, the studio promised to rent a mansion, complete with a full staff, to house the major talent. The rental had three stories on the main house and several buildings scattered on the three-acre property. The region, the location of Jack London's novel, was dotted with large farms and sweeping vistas.

The shot list arranged for them to spend three consecutive months together, a record in recent years. Coop and Sirena could each come and go at various times when they weren't on camera.

The two of them hashed out the details of the shoot before they signed their contracts. Since the accommodations were roomy enough for live-in staff, Sirena insisted that Amelia stay in the main house with her and Coop.

"I thought we would treat this as a second honeymoon, a chance to be together," Coop argued. He paced back and forth in the bedroom in their Italianate mansion in Bel Air.

"We will be together—for ten hours at a time on the set some days. I think this is going to be great for both of us, personally and professionally," she said, nibbling his ear. "You can bring Peter Trent-Jones to pick up your dirty clothes. The studio agreed your valet could accompany us. I want Amelia in the house with us. She's signed on to do hair on the picture, and it will be so much more convenient to have her under the same roof. We'll be on two of the three stories, so there's plenty of room. And Harlow can come too. Amelia will feed her and Trent-Jones can change her litter box."

"Harlow will just get lost, and there are probably coyotes out there. It would be much safer if she stays put in L.A. with Leticia taking care of her at Lion's Lair. We can't leave the house unattended. And you see enough of Amelia as it is right now. I don't particularly want her living with us. The studio can make other housing arrangements for her."

"Do I detect a note of jealousy?" Sirena draped her arms around his neck. "Nobody knows my hair like she does. After all these years, she's my best friend, other than you." Sirena started to unbutton his shirt.

"Okay, just make sure that she's on the other end of the house and on a separate floor, maybe near Trent-Jones. Who knows? They might hook up. But Harlow stays home with Leticia."

"All right, I'll compromise. Thanks, love, you'll probably be sick of our working together stuck out in the boonies for a few months."

"Not a chance. I don't like it when you're out of my sight for even a minute." He drew her closer, wrapping his arms around her.

Sirena gave him a quick kiss and pulled away. She reached for the phone and called Amelia. "Hi, we're in business! Coop said he'd love to have you stay with us." Sirena glanced at her husband and stuck out her tongue.

"Why don't we just have a damned commune," Coop shouted loudly enough for Amelia to hear over the line.

"Is he pissed off?" Amelia asked.

"No, he's not mad," Sirena said into the receiver. "He's just joking around. At least we'll be in California so my hair won't frizz like it does when we're in the South or in tropical locations."

"We make a great team. As long as you keep getting parts, I keep working. That gorgeous head of hair of yours is going to help me earn enough money to buy a house in the Hollywood Hills one day. Thanks for getting the studios to include my services in your contracts," Amelia said.

"The way you always make me look, I'll always want you with me."

"Thanks, hon, I'm counting on that," Amelia said.

"Gotta run. Coop and I have got some things to go over." He stroked her breast and tried to snatch the phone away from her.

"Later," Amelia said and hung up.

"I realize you've known her forever, but I hope you don't tell her everything about us," Coop said.

"I tell Amelia a lot, but there are some things that belong to just us. You know that. I would never ..."

"I'm glad to hear that." Coop guided her onto their bed.

21
SIRENA &
COOP

TO REACH THE COUPLE'S ACCOMMODATIONS during the location shoot for *Big House, Little Lady*, the limo climbed the winding drive toward a sprawling Victorian house perched on the top of a rise. The setting sun sent golden rays peeking through the gingerbread trim.

"I hope there aren't any coyotes roaming around," Sirena said.

"It's the country, babe. Smell the clean air. No smog, no traffic," Coop said.

"I'm going to croak if I don't get a tall latte in the next five minutes."

"Don't be such a diva! Just look at that fruit grove at the end of that green field. You can even smell it from here."

"Oh, so now you're a gentleman farmer? I'll bet you don't even know what's growing in that patch of dirt."

"I read the script. It's alfalfa!"

"The only Alfalfa I know is the funny-looking kid with a cowlick in the *Little Rascals* reruns," Sirena said. The car glided to a stop. "Enough already, let's go inside." She laughed and then gave him a quick peck on the lips.

He grabbed her and held her close. "We're going to enjoy this time together."

The house manager, Christina, opened the door and welcomed the pair. She wore a loose dress that looked hand-loomed. The aroma of coffee floated in the air.

"Now *that's* what I call a great smell," Sirena said, nudging Coop's arm.

"We make a fresh pot of espresso every morning," Christina said. "Also, you can give me your breakfast order before you go to bed. There's a menu, but the chef will whip up anything you want."

Sirena shot a triumphant look at Coop. "That's just perfect. Really, I hate to make y'all go to all that trouble, but I'd love a tall latte now."

Coop headed toward the bedroom, and Sirena stayed downstairs and gushed over the antiques while Christina showed her around the mansion.

Upstairs, Coop plopped onto the four-poster bed to test its firmness and stared up at the antique crystal chandelier casting tiny rainbows across the ceiling. The studio had added requested furnishings and other improvements to Sirena and Coop's temporary home, including a bidet. His cell phone disturbed the quiet.

"Coop, it's Charlie. Ready for company?"

"Yeah, what's up, my little marketing guru?"

"Arthur and I are taking a meeting with your director. We've got to go over Jack Wesson's shot list so we can keep working on the creative materials. We need you and Sirena to take a look at the one-sheet poster layouts."

"Charlie, you're cool, but you better make sure the meeting's short. Fielgood gives me the creeps."

"Are you forgetting something? Like he's my boss," Charlie said.

"I'd rather forget it. He's such a pompous asshole."

"Coop, Arthur knows his marketing, even though he *can* be difficult." Charlie tried to uphold solidarity with her department.

"We all know who does the work and who gets the credit," Coop said. "I'd like to see that change."

"If he's on top, then I'm right there too. Our whole team at Silverlake's working for you," Charlie said.

"Good party line, but I'm not sitting next to that turkey."

"You can sandwich between Sirena and me," Charlie said with a giggle.

"Now that sounds mighty tasty," he said. "But seriously, don't let that schmuck walk all over you."

"No way. We'll be there tomorrow around lunchtime. If I'm lucky, I'll catch the last take on set in the morning. Give Sirena a hug. See you *mañana*."

"Yep."

"*Ciao*." Charlie hung up. She was satisfied that one of Hollywood's biggest stars was singling her out for attention. *Stay a team player and recognition will come in one form or another*, she thought.

Early the next morning, Charlie and Arthur met at the Hollywood Burbank Airport to take a puddle jumper to Sacramento. It dipped and bounced like a paper airplane in the updrafts.

"Damn all those stars! First class isn't good enough for any of them. The company jet is tied up for the press junket in Chicago, and I'm stuck in a crop duster to the capital of Cal-i-for-ni-a." Arthur pronounced the state with an exaggerated German accent. He polished off his second drink.

Charlie nodded and continued to go over her notes. She paused to watch the landscape morph into a yellow, green, and golden patchwork quilt as they approached their destination. She barely felt the plane touch ground on the perfect landing.

Arthur threw off his seat belt. "I can't believe we've got to take this death trap back to L.A."

As she climbed down the stairs of the plane, brisk gusts made Charlie wish she had brought a heavier jacket. Arthur put his arm around her when they reached the tarmac. "I'm fine, really," she said, escaping a few steps ahead of him.

A limo met them at curbside. As soon as they climbed into the back seat, Arthur got on his cell phone. He talked nonstop during the hour drive to the location of the shoot. Charlie edged near the door on her side and tried to plow through the daily deluge of emails on her phone.

The car stopped at the top of an unpaved road that led to nowhere. A young production assistant greeted Charlie and Arthur and guided them toward the *Big House* set—a sprawling structure with an irregular red tile roof that connected various parts of the building. Patios and pergolas punctuated the Hispano-Moresque stucco compound. Towers soared to create height, and sleeping porches offered cool retreats shaded by ancient oaks. Gardens of lilacs and ferns with stone walkways led to hitching posts and gravel paths.

The interior featured a cavernous dining room and an office for main character Dick Forrest with a hidden stairway. A private, elegant spa was located off the separate sleeping quarters for Paula, the Little Lady of the Big House.

Charlie zigzagged on the gravel path to avoid stepping in puddles from the morning downpour. She and Arthur entered the vestibule of the house and stood near a wall of bookshelves that created Dick Forrest's library.

"So how was your flight?" the assistant asked.

"You could hardly call that roller coaster ride a flight," Arthur replied.

"Keep it down! We're still shooting," a crewmember warned.

"Cut!" the director shouted. In an adjacent room, the house exploded with activity. The script girl deposited the pages in the pockets of the directors' chairs, lighting grips wrangled cables, and the camera dolly operator moved across the parlor.

Charlie marveled at the interior of the old mansion that had been converted into Jack London's Big House on a massive ranch. Sirena greeted her and planted a kiss on both cheeks, and Coop hugged her warmly.

"Great to see you, Charlie. Arthur, still keepin' that publicity machine stoked?" he asked.

"Yeah, we're smokin'!" Arthur reached out to shake Coop's hand.

Jack Wesson, the director, stepped between them. "Hi, guys, we're ready for another take. Arthur and Charlie, you two can stick around. You're fine over there." He pointed to a crimson velvet settee in the parlor with open walls so the camera could freely move around the set.

Sirena sat at a concert grand piano on a platform under a low arch at the far end of the music room. She adjusted the seat and positioned her hands on the ivory keys. Amelia placed Sirena's dyed honey-colored tendrils down her back so her face could be visible in the camera angles of the various takes. She gently massaged Sirena's neck to relax her before the shoot. Nearby, a body double with an identical hairstyle and light blue gown with gold trim waited in the wings.

The production assistant signaled it was time to get started. Coop leaned forward to kiss Sirena before they separated to take their marks, as he was to stand near her while she played the instrument.

"Watch my makeup!" Sirena said. She pulled away, adjusting the deep, revealing cowl neckline of her gown.

Coop leaned against a thick column and held a glass with a swallow of whiskey left.

The set quieted down. The clapboard snapped shut.

"Action … and rolling," Jack said smoothly.

The character Paula Forrest masterfully played a final passage of Rachmaninoff's *Prelude in C Sharp Minor*. Her confident fingers flew across the keyboard. The notes faded hauntingly at the end of the vigorous performance and seemed to linger in the air like her perfume.

Sirena had studied for months to be able to ripple her hands over the keys in chords and runs of the complicated score. Close-ups by a professional pianist would be edited in the final cut with the actual music track.

Actor Brent Wilder as Paula's husband, Dick Forrest, clapped heartily from his big koa-wood chair, exclaiming, "She'll run rings around you as far as music theory. The Lady of the House studied with the great Leschetizky. Paula doesn't play like a woman either."

Coop as Graham, the handsome houseguest, couldn't take his eyes off her. "Such power and purity in her interpretation of the music! She can tame stallions and play like a virtuoso."

Paula responded, with sparkling eyes, "We have a new prophet. Thank you, Mr. Graham."

"Is there anything you can't do, Mrs. Forrest?" Graham asked.

"Sleep through the night. We call those bouts of insomnia her 'white nights,'" Dick Forrest added.

"Don't tell all my secrets, my Red Cloud," Paula scolded her husband, using her pet name for him. She stood to gather the sheet music, and Graham moved next to her to close the piano. His hand slid across her arm as he leaned over the musical instrument.

"I've got an early meeting, but why don't the two of you have a nightcap. The servant will refresh your drink, man," Forrest offered in a husky voice.

"Maybe a wee one in a few minutes," Paula said, collecting her empty champagne flute from a side table. "Sleep well, Red Cloud," she said without moving closer to kiss her husband good night.

Forrest left the room alone and lingered beyond the doorway to light a cigarette.

Graham pulled Paula's face close to him, their lips touching and then hungrily kissing her until they had to come up for breath.

Forrest continued down the hall to his bedchamber. Off camera he called out, "Good night, Little Bird-woman."

Graham lifted Paula's gown to see the knees he had remembered from her wild ride in the pond that had been full of foam and fury. He moved his hand beneath her skirt and searched until he touched the silkiness of her body. She didn't wear a confining corset or bulky knickers.

Then he maneuvered her toward the piano bench. His mouth inched down her neck to her breasts that were loosely draped by the bodice of her gown.

Sirena swooned as Coop's hand teased under her skirt.

The body double watched with attention, ready to be called for a close-up in the next scene. The cue didn't come.

Sirena threw her head back in ecstasy.

Coop released a smile he'd never shown to the camera before, the way a man smiles at a memory.

The director yelled, "Cut!"

22

CHARLIE &
ARTHUR

COOP STAYED IN CHARACTER and caressed Sirena tightly after the cameras stopped filming. The stars held a lingering, passionate kiss while the crew members applauded.

"Okay, let's break for lunch!" the director, Jack Wesson, shouted.

The assistant called out, "Everyone back on the set at one fifteen sharp. Let's not make this a three-Cosmopolitan lunch, people."

Jack walked over to Arthur and Charlie sitting knee to knee on the settee. "Ready with the marketing plan?"

Charlie struggled to extricate herself from the low seat and stood to give him a hug. "Ready as we'll ever be."

"We'll kick some ass with this one, Jack," Arthur said. "It'll open number one. I guaran-damn-tee it!"

"Just as long as you spend more than you did on my last flick."

"Every director in Hollywood will be envying you after this budget."

"We'll have a working lunch in the Forrest dining room," Jack said. "Give Sirena and Coop a little time to cool down from their scene.

You need to exit the building where you came in and walk around the east wing."

The two stars sauntered arm in arm out of the Big House, kissing and walking at the same time.

"Guys, if you keep that up, you'll both have to spend a few additional hours in makeup," Jack said playfully.

"Don't mess with my hair," Sirena scolded Coop. "Amelia really got it just right."

"Oh, I thought she *always* works magic on your hair," Coop muttered. "Besides, you're supposed to look tousled after our lovemaking scene." He was getting tired of hearing how Amelia could do no wrong and wished he had not agreed to let her live with them.

"All I've ever heard is that I always look too perfect—even in my last film when I was in the middle of being raped." She pursed her full lips.

"Babe, you can't help that you're a fucking fox."

Sirena's pout turned into a pucker.

Amelia walked over to the pair. "Sirena. I'll check you out after lunch. We'll get together later. Continuity will crucify me if one hair isn't exactly the same as it was in the last take."

"Okay, hon. Wish you could have lunch with us."

"Even in this freakin' farm, there's still a damned A-list," Amelia said, picking up her box of hairbrushes. "I have to eat in the barn where they set up hay bales as seats for the crew except the big shots."

"It's a ranch," Coop said.

"Don't worry. I'll find you after we finish." Sirena walked away with Coop toward his trailer under the oak trees.

"Remember, we're meeting with Arthur and Charlie in the dining room in ten minutes," Jack called to them.

"That should just about give us enough time … to get started," Coop said, patting Sirena's behind in her flowing gown.

"You usually take a little longer," she said.

"I'll show you just how long."

"Ten minutes, everyone!" Jack said as he walked down the gravel path, kicking pebbles with his ostrich-skin cowboy boots.

Charlie struggled to keep pace in her heels.

Charlie, Arthur, and Jack entered the main section of the Big House. For a minute Charlie forgot that it was a motion picture set until she noticed that the right wing of the mansion was completely open in the back. The set designers had taken an existing house and had modified and expanded it for their cinematic needs.

The aroma of roasted garlic permeated the front rooms that were sheltered by a roof. Charlie stopped to sniff the loopy bouquet of wild flowers and examined the antique props in the hutch.

In about a half hour, Coop and Sirena wandered into the kitchen where the chef was tossing Portobello mushrooms, lamb chops, and jumbo shrimp on a commercial stove with a grill.

"Looks great!" he said and gave the cook the thumbs-up.

"Thanks, Mr. Cooper. Brittany will serve you tonight."

"Chef, just call me Coop."

"Okay, Coop. Let's get started. Get in here, you two, please," Jack said as he stuck his head into the kitchen. Coop and Sirena followed Jack and Arthur into the dining room.

Balancing a tray of canapés, Brittany, a curvaceous strawberry blonde, paused and stared at the handsome movie star.

"That platter of jumbo shrimp looks great," Coop said and winked at her.

"I always think jumbo shrimp's an oxymoron," Arthur quipped.

"What? Did someone say something about a moron?" Coop gave Charlie a conspiratorial glance.

"Sirena and Coop, sit on this side near me. Jack and Charlie, over there," Arthur instructed. "Charlie, have you got the materials?"

Coop pulled out a chair for Charlie, and Sirena flanked his other side. Looking like he had just lost a game of musical chairs, Arthur claimed the seat next to the director.

"Let's eat first, and then we'll take a look. Hope they've got some decent wine around here," Coop said.

"We've still got to pick up some shots on the patio before we lose the golden light, so take it easy, kids," Jack warned.

"Well, us adults can knock back a few, right, Jack?" Arthur brushed the director's shoulder.

Coop leaned over and said, "So what kind of marketing plan have you cooked up for us, Charlie?"

"This campaign's going to knock your shorts off," Arthur replied. "From what I've seen from the film clips we used for the teaser trailer, I'll bet the ranch that we'll sweep the Movie Constellation Awards."

"From your lips," Charlie said. She extracted a pile of papers from her briefcase.

The meeting lasted a little under an hour. Sirena pushed around the field greens salad on her plate without actually eating a bite.

"We've got to wrap this up. Call me later and we'll go over the rest of the layouts," Jack said. "Just leave copies on the table."

"That's copasetic! We've hit the broad strokes, and we've lined up some product sponsors," Arthur replied.

"You and Charlie, stay and finish your wine. Coop and Sirena, let's get back to the set, my little lovebirds. I'm losing the light." The director drank the last sip from his goblet.

Coop gave Charlie a hug before he, Sirena, and Jack exited through the open back of the building to reach the patio of the Big House.

"Is there anything else you'd like?" Brittany asked Arthur as she removed the napkin from his lap.

"Got another bottle of that marvelous chardonnay?"

"I'll have to check the wine cellar. It's such a small vineyard that they usually don't produce a lot. But I'll see what we've got in. I'll be back in a minute. And for you, ma'am?"

"Nothing, thanks. I'm fine." Charlie folded her napkin and placed it on the table.

"You certainly are, but that's beside the point," Arthur said. How 'bout that bottle, Brittany?"

"Coming right up, sir." Brittany turned around to see if Arthur was watching her best angle, her well-toned derrière poured into snug jeans.

"Charlie, what's the rush? The day's over already. Enjoy the moment," Arthur toasted, raising his half-full glass.

"I've got to call Gabe to find out if the product tie-in contracts were signed today. I want to hit the ground running on Monday."

"That can wait. It's Friday afternoon. We have plenty of time, and it'd be a miracle if Gabe could get anyone on the line right now," Arthur said with a grin.

"We should be heading back pretty soon." Charlie checked her watch. The empty crystal glasses sparkled in the afternoon sun streaming in from the gap in the wall behind her.

"I could spend a little time up here. Never figured the Sacramento Valley could be a great place for a quick weekend getaway," Arthur said.

"Excuse me for saying this, but I don't think it's really Teeni's scene."

"I know that. How's the scene play with you?"

Charlie scooted her chair to escape from the table. "Arthur, if you mean ..."

"I mean, what did you think of that last scene with Coop and Sirena on the set? What'd you think I meant?"

Charlie stood up and almost collided with Brittany dashing into the room.

"Found it!" the waitress chirped, clutching the wine bottle and a plate of chocolates. "You got lucky. There was only one left."

"No, I *almost* got lucky. We've got to be heading out," he said.

"Well, I'm real sorry to see you go so soon," Brittany said, leaning down to top off his glass.

"Don't worry. I'll be back before they finish filming."

"Oh, Mr. Fielgood, I hope you don't think I'm too forward."

"What's up, kiddo?"

"I've got a script in the kitchen. I was wondering if you'd take a look at it. It's about the hottest girl in Sacramento who gets her big break in Hollywood from a powerful movie executive."

"Sounds promising. I've got to catch a plane, but remind me about it the next time I'm up here for the wrap party in a few weeks." Arthur winked and slowly sank his teeth into a chocolate truffle. "Charlie, give the driver a call."

"Arthur, I'll meet you at the car. Let's compare notes on the way to the airport." Charlie clutched her briefcase and ambled down the dusty path alone, kicking a stone along the way. She had enough on her plate to plan the launch of *Big House, Little Lady*, and Arthur's advances were unwanted distractions.

Even while the film was being shot, the studio had high hopes for it to garner a record number of Movie Constellation Awards. Coop and Sirena's success costarring as a married couple was predicted to make film history.

23
SIRENA

S IRENA TWIRLED A STRAND of her platinum hair, waiting backstage for her entrance cue at the Movie Constellation Awards ceremony. The first three minor prizes had been presented: Art Direction, Makeup, and Score. Each minute she waited seemed to drag by in slow motion. It was almost time to earn the swag-filled goody basket for presenters that cluttered the guest room of her house in the Hollywood Hills.

The audience erupted into cheers when superstar Ricardo Perrino strode across the stage to set up the film clips for one of the Best Picture nominations. He waited for the applause to die down before he began the introduction. The lights dimmed, and *Big House, Little Lady* flashed across the screen.

Sirena was radiant as Paula Forrest; her beauty dominated the film screen. Coop looked virile and handsome, clutching his real-life ex-wife in a passionate embrace. Sweeping vistas of the Sacramento Valley were captured in a montage by the award-winning cinematographer.

When the theater's house lights rose, the crowd clapped wildly in support. Coop leaned over to Francine and whispered, "We've got it made." The camera zoomed in to catch him whispering behind his hand to the older woman at his side, which would probably end up as a clip on entertainment gossip shows wondering who was Coop's mature mystery date.

The momentum of the ceremony halted for a commercial break, and then the low din of conversation in the auditorium steadily heightened. People bolted from their seats for bathroom breaks, and like magic, seat-fillers instantly appeared as surrogate celebrities. Arthur hurried down the aisle to pat Coop on the back. Coop continued talking to Francine, ignoring the insistent tapping on his shoulder. Arthur turned to survey the audience spread behind him and glanced up to wave to Charlie and Gabe seated in the overhanging balcony. At the last moment of warning for the show to begin, Coop turned and shook Arthur's hand. The lights flickered, and Arthur heeded the cue and raced back to his seat, squeezing by the attractive young woman he displaced.

"Thought he'd never go," Francine said.

"Got Mercedes's hotel number?" Coop asked Francine.

"It's after midnight in London."

"Not a problem."

"But the show's about to start. I'll call her first thing in the morning to discuss the results. I'm sure we'll have some good news." Francine clutched Coop's hand.

"You've really got to give Mercedes a raise. Whatever you're paying her, it's not enough," Coop said.

"Believe me, sweetheart, she gets what she deserves."

The music swelled, and a panorama of the audience filled the massive video monitors on each side of the stage. The gilded logo of the Movie Constellation Awards swirled over the image of the glamorous crowd. The announcer's voice boomed, "Everyone, welcome the lovely Little Lady of the Big House, Miss Sirena Jackson."

Sirena glided across the stage, shimmering in her form-fitting blue gown. The audience buzzed with approval. Her sapphire-and-diamond necklace on her down-to-there neckline flashed starbursts in the lens.

A second cameraman crouched in front of Ethan Dean Traynor and captured his wide grin that seemed to proclaim, "I'm the lucky bastard who's sleeping with her."

Sirena approached the microphone, careful to push her shoulders back and her chest forward. She remembered the years of training that had taught her how to avoid looking like a hunchback at a lectern and to speak naturally and not to stoop toward the microphone.

"Some of y'all know that my film is about the age-old struggle with temptation and darker impulses," she said.

A quick close-up of Coop flashed on the huge screens.

Sirena giggled and smoothed her hair. "Sorry, I had to adjust my halo."

"You go, girl!" a woman yelled from the balcony.

Sirena smiled beatifically and continued, "Character actors usually get to show the range of human emotions. I'm honored to present the award for this category. The nominees for Featured Actor in a Supporting Role are ..."

After the clips were shown, Sirena held the envelope up to the lights to feign a sneak peek. She cracked open the wax seal and slowly pulled out a creamy card.

"And this little golden lady, the Constance Award, goes to our very own Brent Wilder, as my on-screen husband, Dick Forrest, in *Big House, Little Lady*."

Brent sprinted onto the stage like an athlete, taking two steps at a time. He clutched Sirena toward him and planted a sloppy kiss on her mouth. She backed away, wiping her lips with her fist. She adjusted her necklace and maintained an impassive look while he thanked the voters in a thick English accent.

In the balcony, Charlie whispered to Gabe, "Those Brits always make the best Americans: Roddy McDowall and Vivien Leigh."

"Yeah, Christian Bale was a great Batman."

"Where does Brent Wilder get off kissing Sirena like that?" Charlie asked.

"Funny, she did look pissed," Gabe said.

"He doesn't really know her; they only worked together. Try that in an office and it would be sexual harassment," Charlie said.

A man behind them said, "If you're so into gossip, go get a tabloid! Zip it!"

"We'll get the full scoop from Sirena at the Constellation Ball," Gabe announced loudly enough for everyone nearby to hear that he was connected to the pulse of Hollywood.

The orchestra started to play softly while Brent pulled out a sheet of paper to check if he had forgotten to thank anyone. He resumed mentioning a list of first names that meant nothing to the viewing public but meant everything to the people who were acknowledged. Then he droned on about his agent who had to help him fight to get the part. The music amplified until it overrode his remarks. Finally the microphone was cut and Brent reluctantly left the stage like a spurned lover. Sirena regally strode in front of him, not waiting to be escorted. Amelia met her in the wings, just offstage.

"What a giant asshole!" Amelia raged.

When Brent walked by, Sirena said, "Who do you think you are, kissing me like that? If you ever so much as look at me again ..."

"I guess I got caught up in the moment."

"Think you're big-time now, huh?" Amelia said.

"I don't think an overweight beautician has much room to talk," Brent snapped.

Amelia lunged forward with her fist clenched.

Sirena grabbed her arm, blocking any contact. "He's not worth it, love."

"He's such a prick," Amelia said, looking away to hide her glassy eyes. "And he has a brassy blond dye job!"

"The only thing hard on him is that hunk of shiny metal he's holding. Let's get out of this hallway." Sirena dabbed a tear from Amelia's cheek.

From backstage, a camera clicked in rapid-fire. Arm in arm, Sirena and Amelia headed toward the dressing rooms.

24
SIRENA &
AMELIA

I N A CLOSE-UP OF THE MOVIE Constellation Awards telecast, Dena
Dearmon clutched the microphone close to her lips, breathily singing "Paula's Love Dilemma," the nominated song for *Big House, Little
Lady*. Midway through the number, Coop brushed Francine's hand
off his arm and left his seat. A man in a tuxedo instantly filled the
vacant spot on the first row.

In the theater lobby, Coop scrolled through his phone log to find
a number with a foreign area code. He pressed Send and hoped his
lover in London would pick up.

"Coop, aren't you still at the ceremony? Good news, I hope,"
Mercedes said.

"Not yet. Dena Dearmon's in the middle of a number, so I ducked
out to give you a call. I don't know why I didn't insist that you come
with me tonight."

"You know I don't want to be at the center of a media frenzy as
Coop's new gal pal. Besides, Francine will make my life miserable if
she finds out," Mercedes said.

"We're not going to have you exiled to Siberia every time I have to attend a gala."

"She certainly was hell-bent to send me to England to check on the Royal Premiere for *Big House*. All of the arrangements were already completed before I arrived. The local guys in the Silverlake office have got everything under control; all the press is lined up. The Queen is supposed to attend this one. The rest of the royal entourage is iffy. It changes daily, but I don't have to be monitoring the RSVP list. I just need to make sure that you'll be here in London with me."

"I'll be there, and so will you. You can count on it!" Coop said.

"Let's hope Teeni doesn't show up and start an international incident with the Queen."

"I think Francine's been taking a few lessons from that spoiled Hollywood wife," Coop said.

"I guess you're right that Francine's doing everything she can to make my life difficult and to keep me as far away from you as possible. I even had to go check on the invitations, hand etched by the royal engraver. Not much room for error there. Didn't she ever hear of using a courier to ship a press proof? Doing grunt work isn't exactly what I expected," Mercedes said.

"I'd like to be doing a little grunt work with you right now—and groaning."

"Hold that thought when I see you next week."

"That's the trouble, I *am* holding it," Coop said and laughed. "Mercedes, I really miss being with you."

"*Moi aussi*, my great big movie star."

The applause from the auditorium drifted into the hallway. "Guess the number's over. I'll call you in a while. Cross your fingers."

"I don't need to. You're a lock."

Coop made his way to his seat just as the music signaled the next award. He glanced across his row and spotted Sirena giggling with

Ethan. He remembered how the bridge of her nose crinkled with her nervous laugh.

Emcee Willy Rivers took the stage again. "The star power in the next award is enough to light up the whole San Fernando Valley in a blackout. Welcome Michael Laniere, recipient of last year's Lead Actor award, to do the honors for the women in a starring role."

Michael's dimples flickered across his face when he read the names of the five nominees. Respectful applause followed the movie scenes of the first four actresses.

Sirena's clip exploded on the screen. With a mighty splash, she rode a stallion that reared upward into the water and then submerged when it lost its footing.

She struggled to right the floundering beast while her husband, Dick Forrest, shouted, "Ride his neck!"

She wordlessly mastered the ruddy bay and shot a triumphant look at the spectators, a group of female friends, her husband, and the mysterious stranger at his side. When the lights came up after Sirena's scene, loud cheers rocked the room.

The camera panned to each of the nominees. A close-up caught Sirena twisting a lock of her hair for good luck.

Michael coyly tossed the envelope from hand to hand. "I'll announce the winner if I can get a whopping kiss like Brent Wilder got. No seriously, folks, the Lead Actress award goes to …" He fumbled with the card. "I knew it! Sirena Jackson, that gorgeous Little Lady with huge talent from *Big House, Little Lady*!"

Sirena covered her face in mock disbelief. She kissed Ethan on the lips and then smoothed her hair, tussled from his embrace. She slowly glided to the podium as if it were her coronation. Her long train swept behind as she made her way up the glowing staircase.

The crowd rose, clapping and cheering. Sirena repeatedly thanked the audience, shifting her stance from leg to leg. Her eyes glistened with building emotion.

Close-ups captured the other four nominees smiling with their mouths only, their eyes flat.

Michael handed the gold-plated statue to Sirena. She hoisted it high above her head and waved it from side to side. "Working out for this part included daily weight training, so this six-pound little lady's nothing for me to lift," Sirena said. Then she cradled the statue like a baby. "None of you will ever know what this means to me. From the time I was a girl in Marietta, Georgia, I dreamed of being in the movies. When the amazing Jack Wesson asked me to play Paula Forrest, he saw something in me that even I didn't know existed."

Jack modestly smiled and gave her a short salute.

"I had to reach down and imagine a person who flaunted the conventions of society, who followed her heart against all odds, and wasn't overshadowed by her powerful husband," she said, with narrowed eyes fixed on Coop.

He stared intently ahead.

"I'd like to thank my brilliant costar Brent Wilder; Manny Silverstein at Silverlake, who's the best Motion Picture Chairman ever. Uh, Carl Atkins in production, Arthur Fielgood, Charlie Wallach and the rest of the marketing team, and of course, the real creator of this phenomenal work—Jack London," Sirena said as her hazel eyes looked skyward.

The music began to swell in the background.

"I'm not getting off this stage before I thank the person who keeps me going in this crazy life I live: Amelia Patterson."

Sirena started to exit the stage when she noticed her date, Ethan, with an unsettled look on his face. She turned back toward the microphone, but the golden-gowned usher led her toward the wings. "Oh my God, I forgot to thank ..." she muttered.

Sirena turned and blew a kiss to Ethan. He shrugged and then smiled, relieved slightly that she had also failed to mention Coop.

Down the hallway lined with award logos, Sirena joined the group of the night's previous winners. Brent Wilder started to congratulate her, but he reconsidered after Sirena's glare warned him to keep his distance.

Sharon Roundtree from the *Movie Times Journal* elbowed her way closer to Sirena. "What did you want to say when they whisked you offstage?"

"I'll never be able to make this up to him, Ethan Dean Traynor. He's gotten me through some tough times lately."

"And what about your costar and ex-husband, Preston Cooper?"

"I can't believe that I left him off too. I was so stunned by the moment; you have no idea. The women in my acting category were so deserving that I didn't write down anything in advance. Coop was fantastic as Evan Graham, and he gave me someone to play against. He and the director Jack Wesson let me run wild with the part. There was much more than learning to ride a horse! Oh my God, I'm sure I left off dozens of other people. I even forgot to mention that I promised my limo driver a dozen hamburgers if I won!"

"Tell me about the woman you mentioned."

"Amelia Patterson and I have been together since we were kids in Georgia. She's my hairstylist and much more."

Sirena heard the squeal before she saw Amelia. They hugged and jumped up and down, crying and laughing like schoolgirls. Amelia got tangled in the train of Sirena's gown as they swirled around. Sirena laughed as they struggled to regain their balance.

The photographers jostled for position. Amelia finally released Sirena, who slid her arm halfway around Amelia's ample waist.

Then Sirena planted one hand on her hip and held up the Constance statue. The cameras clicked in a frenetic staccato. "Thanks, guys, let's take five. I've got to do a hair and makeup check," Sirena pleaded. She took Amelia's hand and led her toward the dressing room.

In the dimly lit hallway, they hugged again. "Honey, let me *really* thank you," Sirena said. She bent down and lifted Amelia's face to hers, and they shared a passionate, familiar kiss. Their mouths celebrated each other's attraction and excitement. Still in their embrace, they heard voices coming toward them. Amelia wiped her lips with the back of her hand to remove the blur of Sirena's red lipstick, but her sweet taste remained. As voices seemed to get closer, the pair hurried down the hall.

25
COOP &
FRANCINE

I N THE DISTANT VIEW from the upper balcony at the awards ceremony, Charlie had watched Sirena appear as a glittery blue speck
in a sea of gold on stage.

"We surrendered our orchestra seats so Brent Wilder could bring
his whole entourage. I work too hard all year to be stuck up here in
the nosebleed section," Charlie vented.

"I'm just happy to be here at all. It's much better than watching it
at home on television," Gabe said. He thumbed through his program
to see how many awards were left to be presented.

"You're such a candy ass!" She gave him a quick pinch on the
stripe of his tux pants. "I guess someone around here's got to be a
goody-goody. At least Brent won, so our sacrifice wasn't in vain."

"On the bright side, we've got a sweet table at the Constellation
Ball, so you'll get some face time when it counts," Gabe said. "I took
a look at our table on the seating chart. Not bad."

"Yeah, if any of the stars stay there long enough to get to see them before they head out to the after-parties. And our department pays hundreds of dollars a pop for them to stick their heads in for five minutes," Charlie said. "I guess if the press gets a few shots of them at the ball, that's the value of the empty seat."

"You always tell me that it's part of the game."

"Gabe, I always say you're a quick study!" Charlie gave him a pat on the back.

The commercial break at the Movie Constellation Awards ceremony ended, and the crowd settled down again. Coop returned to his row, and the seat-filler vacated his spot and dashed up the aisle.

"Glad you made it back in time. Your award category is up next. I have a good feeling this is going to be your night," Francine said and grabbed his hand.

"Yeah, I wouldn't want to live it down for years like that actress who was a no-show when her name was called. At least I would have been on the phone and not on the crapper like she was," Coop said. He adjusted his arm, and Francine's hand fell limply in her lap.

"Anything important?" she asked.

"Yeah. Mercedes."

"Is everything okay in London? Is there something I should know about?" Francine's creased forehead revealed her worry.

"Mercedes said things are a bit too fine. I want to know why you're always shipping her off to somewhere these days." Coop locked eyes with Francine.

"If you think traveling to London, one of the greatest destinations in the world, is getting rid of someone, I'm sorry. Coop, can we talk about this later? This is *your* moment."

"Just tell me what's going on between the two of you," Coop said.

"I hate to let you know now, but I'm thinking about letting her go. She's not taking her work seriously enough." Francine toyed with the diamond star around her neck.

"Believe me, we *will* talk about this later, *sweetheart*," Coop said and shifted in his seat.

"I really didn't mean to upset you right before your category is announced. Forgive me?"

Coop faced forward, presenting his trademark smile in case the cameras panned his way.

Show host Willy Rivers returned to the stage wielding a rhinestone baseball bat. "Anyone want to get up for a seventh-inning stretch? Yeah, I can see all of you folks belting out the song 'Take Me Out to the Ball Game.' This program's lasting so long we might still be on the air for baseball season." The orchestra played a few electronic organ notes that fizzled like a stale bottle of beer.

"To present our next award, welcome star of stage and screen, two-time Movie Constellation Award-winning actress Merrilee Henderson." The orchestra swelled during the applause.

Merrilee took a low bow. She adjusted her strapless gown that sagged precariously with her full breasts exposed just above her nipples. "Those special words, 'Movie Constellation Award-winning,' added to my name mean so much to me. I know one of these fabulous guys is going to feel the same way. Now watch the clips of five of the most talented—and handsome—men in the industry."

Clean-cut Kramer Knight grinned for the camera after being shown as a ruthless Russian soldier in Afghanistan. Conrad Carter clowned in a close-up after scenes from his dark comedy, *In the Nick of Crime*. Isaac Polk nodded solemnly at the end of his grueling scene from *Underground Railroad Station Stories*. The room erupted for Alan Wise as a dirty cop with a conscience in *Shakedown Showdown*.

Then Coop's scene as Evan Graham from *Big House, Little Lady* appeared. His artful portrayal of a seductive dreamer left the room in a hush, before the applause rippled and then roared through the auditorium. Coop winked at the camera and flashed a wide grin.

Merrilee ripped open the envelope and let out a yell. "He's done it again! The Lead Actor Movie Constellation Award goes to Isaac Polk!"

Isaac sat frozen in his seat, stunned for about five seconds. His wife planted a big kiss and nudged him to get up. Finally he loped toward the stage to accept his award.

Francine turned to Coop, but he remained steadfast and listened intently to Isaac's acceptance speech.

"And in closing, I couldn't be in better company than with the four other guys who were nominated. Coop, your performance set the bar unbelievably high. This statue really should be yours, man."

Coop shook his head in humble disagreement to Isaac's remarks. He imagined Mercedes watching the telecast at that very moment in London. To send her a special sign, he pressed two fingers to his lips.

Willy Rivers returned on stage. "Well, I didn't know that Isaac and Coop have got a thing going. A little wave would have been enough, guys."

Coop laughed and blew Willy a kiss.

The awards ceremony trudged toward the last two major categories. Jack Wesson picked up the Best Director award, and the Las Vegas odds-on favorite, *Big House, Little Lady*, garnered the final prize of the evening: the Movie Constellation Award for Best Picture.

The press swarmed Coop as he headed toward the Constellation Ball.

"What's it like to be shut out?" Microphones hovered in front of his face.

"You were robbed!" an onlooker shouted. The crowd jostled to get closer.

Judy Simmons cornered Coop, blocking his path with her imposing figure. "The picture virtually swept the awards, but you were ignored. How do you feel about it?" A firestorm of camera flashes illuminated the star.

Francine intervened to deftly usher Coop through the chaos of the crowded hallway.

Coop stopped short. "Francine, I'll get in touch with you in a few days."

"What's going on?" she asked, chewing on the tip of the earpiece of her eyeglasses.

"London."

"What about Jack London?"

"I'm catching the next plane to London."

"You can't blow off the Constellation Ball," she said, reaching for his arm.

"Just watch me." He pulled his "not so lucky" limo ticket out of his pocket and headed for the exit.

26
CHARLIE &
GABE

AT THE CONSTELLATION BALL after the awards ceremony, Charlie and Gabe wandered through the maze of tables. The room glittered with golden festoons and cascades of yellow orchids and roses.

"We'd better have a good spot in here to make up for our shitty seats at the ceremony. Hey, you've got to try one of these," Charlie said, snatching a star-shaped cracker heaped with beluga caviar from a silver tray passed by a tuxedoed waiter.

"Never could stand the taste of fish. No way," Gabe said, making a schoolboy grimace.

"Just when I thought you were a grown-up!"

Charlie and Gabe worked the room, talking to stars and executives, as they searched for their table near the fifteen-piece orchestra. "Not bad," Charlie said. She checked the place cards and discovered she was to be seated next to Brent Wilder. "Think he'll give me a great big smooch like he did with Sirena? These days I'd go for almost anyone."

"Been a dry spell?" Gabe asked.

"Like the Santa Ana winds. How about you?"

"Who could get a date with our twenty-four seven schedule?" Gabe asked.

"Yeah, all I ever see are people at work," Charlie said. "I wonder if I'm ever going to find someone to go out with who will put up with my demanding job. There's barely a minute for myself, much less to date."

"I can't imagine that you'd have any trouble! You're a catch." Gabe gave her a thumbs-up.

The table began to fill, like jewels mounted in an expensive setting. Brent arrived with his girlfriend, daughter, and yoga coach—and his new best friend: a shiny Constance statuette. Jack Wesson seated his wife, whom no one bothered to find out her first name or interests. Mrs. Wesson signaled the waiter to keep filling her wineglass.

Heads swiveled, looking around the room at the massive gathering of movie stars and executives. The orchestra played with a sultry singer belting out big band tunes.

"Hard not to dance to this song," Charlie said.

"I'll be your Fred if you'll be my Ginger." Gabe took her hand and led her to the black-and-white checkered dance floor. The musicians finished playing a vintage boogie-woogie that flowed into a sensuous ballad. Gabe removed his glasses and pulled Charlie close to him. She sensed his warm breath on her neck, and his close beard scratched her cheek like pinpricks. She felt the bulge on his well-built body as his hands drifted below her waist.

Charlie pushed away and stopped dancing midway through the song. "Let's get back to the table. It looks like people are already starting to scatter."

Sirena arrived late to the Constellation Ball, finally escaping the siege of reporters backstage. An usher led her, along with Ethan and Amelia, to Arthur's table at the front of the room near the bandstand. Tables hosted by other studio executives entertaining their pictures' stars surrounded them.

Charlie navigated her way through the jumble of sash-draped chairs to congratulate Sirena with a warm hug.

"Charlie, thanks again for all your hard work on *Big House, Little Lady*," Sirena said.

"Nice of you to give me a public shout-out. My family was probably thrilled to hear my name on television," Charlie said.

As Arthur stood to greet Charlie, she reached to shake his hand, but he leaned forward and kissed her hard on the mouth. "We did it, kiddo! I bet the ranch it was going to sweep of all the major categories."

Charlie quickly wiped her lips, exchanging glances with Gabe.

Teeni glared as if her fiery stare could bore a hole through Charlie. "Well, almost a clean sweep. Funny how the leading man was overlooked. Has anyone seen Coop?"

"Bottoms up!" Sirena said, and she and Amelia abruptly left the table. They disappeared into a group of celebrities.

"Nice move, Tee." Arthur snatched Teeni's champagne glass out of her hand. She replaced it with one next to her, even though it had a different shade of lipstick on the rim.

Within half an hour, most of the major stars had disappeared from the gala to grace the after-parties. They were scurrying to arrive at their next destination while the red carpet media coverage was in full force for the award winners at the Constellation Ball.

Charlie and Gabe sat abandoned at their table, dismembering and munching on chocolate Constance Awards dusted with edible metallic gold powder and sugar rhinestones. "Look at all of these desserts that haven't been touched. I don't want to even think of the calories in this statue's pedestal. It's sinful," Charlie said between bites.

"I'll have to spend an extra hour in the gym." Gabe patted his flat stomach.

"Hell, you look buff. It's not going to make an ounce of difference on you. Besides, men drop weight like it's nothing."

"That's what women think."

"Grab a couple of those yummy awards, and let's call it a wrap," Charlie said. "Gabe, page the limo driver."

"Whatever you say, Ms. Wallach."

"Get your tush in gear. Make it snappy!" she commanded with a grin. "The line is going to be ferocious, so text me when our driver shows up."

The rain had subsided to a gentle mist, wrapping Hollywood in a scrim that diffused the beams of the klieg lights. Gabe handed his ticket to the traffic director wearing a slicker. With five-inch stilettos in hand, a starlet stood in line next to him waiting for her ride.

The limo line: the great equalizer, Gabe thought. *Everyone, no matter how big a star, has to wait for their ride to pick them up.*

He notified Charlie when their long black car pulled up to the curb. She stopped to chat with the shoeless glittery starlet and then slid across the plush leather seat next to Gabe.

Shouting over the orchestra had strained Charlie's voice and fatigue set in like the comedown after a wedding that had been in the works for months. She laid back her head, closed her eyes, and listened to the soothing jazz instrumentals in the rolling cocoon.

After a while, the car eased onto Burton Way on the fringe of Beverly Hills. A canopy of palm trees spilled over the side street near the entrance to her condo.

"Want me to walk you to the door?" Gabe asked.

"No, you're off duty now. Good job, Gabe. You've cut your teeth on your first Movie Constellation Awards night!"

"Yeah, for a while there I thought we were going to drown in the storm," Gabe said.

"My heels did! See you early tomorrow morning. The awards-show analysis is in the Camelot conference room at seven."

Gabe leaned over and pecked Charlie on the cheek.

"Don't worry about paying the driver. Everything's taken care of—tip and all," she said. Charlie headed toward her front door. The limo sped off into the night toward Venice Beach to deliver Gabe to his tiny apartment on a canal.

As Charlie unsnapped her purse to get her key, her senses jolted from the smell of fetid breath behind her.

"No key. Get in the car!"

Charlie turned to see a stubbled face with narrow dark eyes inches from hers. A sheepskin vest with no shirt barely covered his bony chest, and he wore a pair of ragged shorts. She shivered from the damp cold and from the dangerous stranger next to her.

Charlie couldn't see a gun, but it seemed like the man meant for her to do as he said.

"You Hollywood Jews! You spread your unholy word in your filthy movies. You like to call the shots. Now I tell you what to do. Into the car!" he snarled.

Charlie tried to think of ways to avoid getting into the battered car. *Where was the private patrol, and how did this madman know she was Jewish?* she wondered. A guy who looked like a maniac sheepherder was accosting her, and the street was deserted without any law enforcement in sight.

"The Jews control everything. *He* commanded it is time for change."

"Who told you that?" she asked.

"I received the word from Him."

Charlie knew when the voice of God, any god, tells someone to act strangely, it's a powerful and frightening sign. "Maybe I can help you get your kind of movies made. Ones that you think are important. How's that sound?"

"More lies. Get into the car—now!" he shouted. He shoved her and she stumbled, hitting the concrete hard on one knee that exploded in pain.

"Get up, whore!"

Charlie stayed hunkered down, hoping to stall for time before he tried to force her into his car.

Suddenly a swirl of blue lights swept the side of the building. A patrol car fishtailed onto her street from Burton Way. Charlie crawled toward the bushes, trying to shield herself. The branches tore her skin, but she pressed closer for cover.

From two directions, officers with drawn guns surrounded the man. "Arms in the air! Now!"

The man ignored the order and bolted toward his car.

"Police! Freeze! Stop where you are right now!"

The man turned and faced the police officers. His crooked grin dominated his defiant look. Then the intruder turned and glared at Charlie huddled in the mildewed mulch. He slowly raised his hands above his head, never removing his eyes from her.

"You belong in the dirt, woman. You and your Jewish kind."

A female officer ran to aid Charlie. "Are you injured, ma'am?" She reached down to help Charlie get to her feet.

"Yes, a little. I landed hard on my left knee, but I think I can walk." Charlie saw a trail of blood trickling down her leg.

One by one, the windows in the condo building lit up like a checkerboard. Silhouettes pressed against the glass and peered onto the street. Her next-door neighbor dashed out the front door in her nightgown.

"Stay back, miss!" an officer commanded, waving to signal a retreat.

The neighbor returned to safety inside, peeking through a narrow transom to get a look at her friend.

The man was read his rights and was shoved into a patrol car, his dirty head carefully shielded by a clutching hand of a police officer.

"Do you know this guy?" the female officer asked.

"This is like some cop show. I can't believe this is happening to me," Charlie muttered.

"Do you know him?"

"Never saw him before in my life. He knew I worked for a studio. Said something about hating Hollywood Jews." Charlie's cell phone rang. "May I answer it?"

The officer nodded, and Charlie's hand trembled while she took the call.

"Are you still up?" Gabe asked.

"You might say so. You're never going to believe this one."

27
CHARLIE

G ABE ARRIVED AT CHARLIE'S CONDO dressed in his tux pants, a
white T-shirt, and a leather jacket he had thrown on after they
spoke on the phone. The female officer let him into the building and
escorted him up the elevator to the unit on the third floor. The curtains were drawn on the windows that usually overlooked a ribbon of
headlights on the wide boulevard of Burton Way. Charlie sat huddled
on the couch, legs drawn up beneath her like a little girl, hidden under
a cashmere throw.

"I'm okay. For God's sake, don't fuss over me," she said with a
gravelly voice.

"How'd that guy find you?" Gabe asked, taking a seat next to Charlie.

"Just lucky, I guess," she said, trying to lighten the moment.

Gabe picked up his ringing phone. "Hi, Arthur. I think she's okay.
I'll put her on."

"You all right, kiddo?"

"Arthur, funny how some people really know how to ruin an evening. Yeah, I'm not really hurt. Though my stockings have seen better days and there's a nasty scratch on my knee. Mainly, I'm just creeped out."

"I'm sending Jamaal Kenter to stay at your place tonight. You need some security. He's through with the Movie Constellation Awards ceremony duty, and I can tell him to drop over."

"I'm not sleeping with some stranger in my house. Can we talk about security tomorrow?" Charlie asked.

"Jamaal's no stranger. Want us to put you up in a hotel?"

"Not really. Let me get some sleep." For a moment Charlie wondered if she had been too gruff. "Thanks, Arthur. I really do appreciate your concern."

"I can be right over if you need me," he said in a sultry voice.

"Oh Lord no! The police officers want to see me in the morning, so I'll be late for the awards postmortem meeting."

"Don't say that word, 'postmortem.' I'm just glad you're safe. Take the day off," Arthur said.

"We'll see. I've got a full plate at the studio. I should be there."

"Gabe'll fill you in. Take it easy, kiddo. I'll check on you later," Arthur said.

"Arthur, really …"

He hung up. Gabe took the phone from Charlie.

"Show up in the morning at the precinct, Ms. Wallach, to go over the incident report. Do you know where to go?" The officer zipped her jacket and headed for the door.

"Yes, right down the street. I can't begin to thank you enough." Tears welled in Charlie's eyes.

"Glad this one had a good ending. Be sure and lock up tight." The officer left, and Gabe flipped the dead bolt.

"For once, Arthur's right. You shouldn't be alone tonight," Gabe said as he sat back down beside her on the couch. He put his arm around her and drew her close.

"Why? What's going to happen? They got the guy," Charlie said, easing into the safety of someone being with her.

"You're still in shock. I'll sleep in the guest room in case you need something, Charlie. You know that line about whistling if you need me, right?"

A smile flashed across her face, the first one since Gabe had arrived. Charlie got up and headed for her bedroom, limping slightly on her left leg. She teetered and skimmed the wall. Gabe jumped up to grab her waist to steady her. "I guess since you're staying, could you bring me a little ice for my knee?"

"I'll bring you whatever you need," he said, pulling her closer.

"A little ice will do just fine."

At the studio the next morning, Jamaal faced Arthur enthroned at his massive desk. The sun struggled to peek through the overcast sky while the rain threatened to persist. Arthur leaned back in his bulky chair until it reached a precarious angle. He closed his eyes and listened to Jamaal's update.

"This guy's seen trouble before. Got a record," Jamaal reported.

"So what's this dirtbag got to do with Charlie?" Arthur looked at his watch and began to click through his online calendar.

"He must have been checking her out, or maybe someone he knows has some beef with her. I don't think the police can hold him on much because he didn't have a weapon. He's some kind of a head case," Jamaal reported.

Arthur barked, "I don't care what he is; we need to ramp up the security around here. Let's make sure he's not working with an accomplice."

"I already alerted the guards at all the entrance gates to the studio." Jamaal moved to the window and scanned the street below.

"There are too many nutjobs running around out there. We need to get some extra protection for Charlie," Arthur said.

"Yeah, man. Got that right. I'll get a bodyguard for her," Jamaal said.

He called Charlie and laid out his plan. She clinched the phone and shouted, "There's no way in hell I'm having a stranger shadow me."

"Okay, let me know if you change your mind," Jamaal said.

Charlie phoned Gabe at the studio. The sound of his voice comforted her, even though he seemed preoccupied. "Thanks for staying over last night. I didn't realize I needed the company."

While he talked, Gabe arranged the papers on his desk, lined up his pencils in a row, and circled in red ink the day's date on his calendar. "You said you needed me, and I was glad to help."

"*You* said I needed you. Thanks," Charlie said. "I've got to go see the Beverly Hills cops. Call you later."

"You'll get a blow by blow of the Movie Constellation Awards meeting, so don't worry. I won't leave out any colorful 'Arthurisms.'" Gabe adjusted his glasses and then jotted down a few lines in the margin of the calendar.

"Can't wait. *Ciao*," Charlie said. "Oh, one more thing—your support means so much to me. Remember what I told you before: I cherish the real friends I've made in this industry."

28
CHARLIE &
ARTHUR

C HARLIE SPENT MOST OF THE MORNING at the police precinct and
didn't make it to the office because she had to go to the doctor in
the afternoon to take care of the festering wound on her knee.

Gabe had called to brief her on the post-Movie Constellation
Awards plans to give *Big House, Little Lady* a boost. Distribution
snagged five hundred more theaters, and newspaper ads were
being satellited to the publications with huge banners that pro-
claimed the impressive award count—a sweep except for the Lead
Actor category.

When she arrived at the office the next day, Charlie received word
that Gabe had called in sick. She planned to contact him to find out
how he was but first scrolled through the list of messages he had pri-
oritized for her return. One day away from the office and her emails
hovered close to one hundred. The phone interrupted her deliberation,
and she picked up the flashing interoffice line.

"Got to talk to you. Something's up," Arthur said.

"When? If it's about that nut, can it wait? I'm up to my ears…"

"No, you better get in here right now, and let's get it over with."

"Give me five." Charlie hung up. She made a mental list of what could be the problem. She didn't think she was being admonished because the studio had fared well at the Movie Constellation Awards; Coop seemed happy to be working with her; and all her ducks seemed to be fairly lined up.

Charlie lingered at Arthur's secretary's desk. "He's ready to see you. Go right in," Amy said.

Charlie entered the corner office and waited for her cue to sit down.

"Close the door, kiddo." He buzzed Amy. "Hold my calls. We don't want to be disturbed."

Charlie sat in a sculptural leather chair. Arthur came out from behind his monolithic desk and took the matching seat facing her.

"Charlene, we've got a situation here."

"Charlene? Are you okay, Arthur? Why so formal all of a sudden?"

"You know there are rules about sexual conduct in the workplace."

Charlie sat quietly. *Finally he's going to apologize after all these years*, she thought.

"Charges of sexual harassment have been brought forward," he said.

Charlie tried to maintain a neutral expression. She wished the door was open and some other executive or someone from human resources was with them. "Arthur, should the two of us be discussing your behavior without a mediator?"

"I think it's in your best interest to keep this between us and the legal department, of course. This is about charges against *you*—not me!"

"Against *me*? Are you joking?" Charlie blurted, her face reddening. "Who's bringing charges?"

"Gabe has filed a sexual harassment claim against you, his immediate supervisor."

The color drained from her face. She sank back in the chair and sat with her mouth agape, shaking her head.

"He said you have made numerous inappropriate advances and constantly commented on his buff physique. He knew details about your bedroom."

"That lying sack of shit. He brought me an ice pack when I split my knee. You know it's not true."

"He has a calendar with dates of the alleged incidents circled in red. He claimed you told him that your vagina was high and dry. The good thing is that he doesn't have any tapes, so it's his word against yours."

"This is just so sick," Charlie said. A bead of sweat formed on her brow. "We were talking about the women's products he had marketed before he came here, not *my* body!"

"He also said you groped him while dirty dancing at the Movie Constellation Ball. I know it's a fucking hot mess, but there's much more."

"He grabbed me! I had to leave the dance floor to get away from him and that day-old scratchy beard. What a crock! And, Arthur, you'd better be more careful with your language. So what does he want?"

"Your job."

Charlie stood up and began to pace, heat rising to her temples. Arthur started to put his arm around her but then stopped and retreated behind his desk.

"Kiddo, you know I don't believe a single word of it. He also says he wants four weeks of vacation and demands two main floor seats at the Constance Awards every year," Arthur said. "He shot himself in the groin with that one; those seats are really golden."

"That little snake! You *do* believe I'm innocent, don't you?"

"Sure, I'm on your side."

"So what's our plan of attack?" Charlie asked.

"I've got to finish talking it over with legal. There's no way he's going to continue at Silverlake Pictures. We'll make some kind of settlement."

"I certainly couldn't work with that little snot after this," Charlie said.

"Gotta keep your nose clean, kiddo. Messy business, this harassment stuff."

"And what do I say to him when he comes back to work?"

"Legal informed Gabe that he's on paid leave until this is resolved," Arthur said. "Go ahead and get out of here for a few days until we put out this fucking fire, but don't take any of the files with you on your way out."

A SEARING RAY BOUNCED OFF the golden Constance statuette on the fireplace mantle. Amelia squinted as the Southern California sunlight streamed in from the French doors overlooking the pool with the Hollywood Hills creating a postcard-perfect backdrop.

"Move a little to your left, Amelia. Sirena, chin down, please. That glass on the coffee table is in my shot," the photographer said.

"Don, can you get them sitting closer together?" Sharon Roundtree from the *Movie Times Journal* asked.

"I know. Vertical layout for the cover. Sharon, you write and I'll shoot," Don said.

"Don't mind him. We're like an old married couple. We've been working together for ten years. How long have the two of you known each other?" Sharon asked, clicking on her tape recorder. "I'm getting this on record."

"Since we were girls in Marietta, Georgia," Sirena relied. "So not that long!"

"You mentioned Amelia in your acceptance speech. What's all that about?"

"I meant what I said. She's always been there for me. Men *come*—and men go." Sirena giggled. "As I was saying, we've always been together."

"What about you, Amelia? What's it like to have one of the world's biggest stars as your BFF?"

"When it's just us, everything's the same as when we were kids growing up together. We still have fun and goof around a lot."

"Don, keep shooting while we're talking," Sharon said without taking her eyes off the pair.

"No candids. Tell me when you're ready for another pose." Sirena puckered her full lips into a sexy, pouty smile.

"So the two of you live together in this fabulous house in the Hollywood Hills. How'd that happen?"

"When I moved out from Lion's Lair, I needed a place that reflected who I am now, not who I was when I was married to Coop. I was so into the palatial scene in Bel Air with crystal chandeliers and huge rooms for entertaining, that this time I wanted something that was intimate and private—and eco-friendly. We've got solar heating panels on the roof and all kinds of energy-saving stuff. There's a fantastic 360-degree view from our hilltop, and we can see the ocean on a clear day. The natural light flooding in keeps up my spirits," Sirena said, flashing a sunny smile. "Unfortunately, Coop got custody of Harlow, our Turkish Angora cat. After a while, I didn't like living alone in this house, so I asked Amelia if she wanted to move in with me. As y'all can see, there's more than enough room."

Sharon scribbled in her notebook. "And how's it working out, Amelia?"

"We're like two peas in a pod. Oh, please don't write that down. I sound like a hick, even though I've lived in L.A. for years."

Suddenly a white ball of fur jumped onto the couch and landed between Sirena and Amelia. Sirena cradled the cat in her arms. "After

I won the Movie Constellation Award for Lead Actress, Coop had his valet deliver her to me as a present with a note of congratulations saying, 'Harlow misses her mother.'"

"Classy touch. Forgive me, but back to where we were before Harlow made her grand entrance: There have been rumors swirling around about the two of you—that you're more than friends." She waited for a reaction, staring into Sirena's legendary hazel eyes.

"We *are* more than friends; we're like sisters," Sirena said, leaning slightly toward Amelia. Sirena took a sip of her soft drink.

"And there are pictures that show you're actually more than sisters."

"What? Which photos?" Sirena calmly placed her glass on the coffee table.

"I've seen them, and they're going to hit the tabloids next week. Might as well tell me, the legitimate press, about what's going on," Sharon said, her eyes fixed on the two women.

"What do they show?" Sirena asked.

"The two of you lip-locked in a hallway, with a Constance statue in your hand. We're not talking about a sisterly smooch here. How long have the two of you been a couple?"

Amelia took a swig from Sirena's glass. She started to sweat and then turned as pale as the cat. "I'll be right back, y'all." At first she slowly sauntered, then she broke into a sprint toward the powder room.

"Like I said—always," Sirena responded.

The sound of Amelia desperately retching was impossible to ignore, spilling over the New Age music that filled the air.

"Think you should check on her?" Sharon asked.

"No, it's the usual these days. That's what happens when there's a pea in a pod."

"Sirena, are you saying …?"

"I'm saying we're going to have a baby," Sirena announced with a genuine, open smile.

Don fumbled his handheld flash unit, and it plummeted to the floor. "Oh shit!"

"That's exactly what Amelia's going to say when she gets back in here and hears I've let the cat out of the bag." Sirena laughed and stroked the white ball of fluff. "Sorry, Harlow, I didn't mean you."

After a few flushes, Amelia emerged looking spent and embarrassed. The others stared at her.

"What? I just lost my cookies. No biggie," she said, returning to her place on the couch.

"They know, honey," Sirena said.

"Know what, for Pete's sake?"

"Everything," Sirena said and kissed Amelia's damp cheek.

Sharon Roundtree's scoop in the *Movie Times Journal* fueled Tinseltown's gossip mill: If Sirena was gay, did that mean that Coop had been in the closet, too, all these years? Was theirs a marriage of convenience, a sham? Talk shows, cocktail parties, carpoolers, and movie moguls speculated about Coop's and Sirena's sex lives separate and together. The tabloids chose the lowest road, maintaining their position as bottom feeders in the publishing world. The Internet exploded, and TV entertainment tabloids led with the story night after night.

Sirena and Amelia had explained in the interview in the *Movie Times Journal* that they wanted their life together to be permanent. They felt a child would secure their bond, and they planned to marry.

Sirena had said, "Coop and I never wanted to have kids. We liked our life the way it was—free to go and do whatever we wanted."

"So what changed?" Sharon asked.

"Amelia and I are forever. Besides, she agreed to carry the baby—to gain all of that weight."

"No one has even noticed that I'm at the end of my second trimester," Amelia said with a grimace. And let's be honest, I'm not on everyone's radar screen like she is."

"Yeah, when I was with Coop, if the slightest wrinkle of my dress flared over my midriff, the tabloids used to have a field day claiming proof that I was pregnant."

"Amelia and I tried IVF three times. It was so hard on us." Sirena squeezed Amelia's fleshy hand.

"Thank goodness, the in vitro finally worked and we're having twins," Amelia said, looking down with pride at her protruding stomach.

"So who's the biological mother?" Sharon asked.

"We don't know, and we've decided to never find out. Guess we'll have a clue if the babies look like either of us, particularly the color of their eyes!" Sirena said.

"I just hope they look like her and not me." Amelia muttered.

"Stop that crap! You're perfect and I love you just the way you are." With her perfectly manicured hand, Sirena caressed Amelia's burgeoning belly. "But better that *you* have the stretch marks than me!"

Sharon inched her chair slightly closer. "And who's the father?"

Sirena met her interviewer's intense gaze. "We're not telling who donated those little swimmers, but I *can* guarantee it wasn't an actor."

Ethan Dean Traynor handled the news as if Sirena had never meant anything to him. He was spotted the next day, lunching in Malibu with a blond starlet with an uncanny resemblance to Sirena.

Coop remained in London—unavailable for comment.

30
COOP &
MERCEDES

T HE INTERNATIONAL GOSSIP PRESS didn't waste any time spreading the word. Amelia and Sirena's kiss backstage at the Movie Constellation Awards was plastered across tabloids throughout the world.

Coop and Mercedes spent the first day of the media blitzkrieg encamped in their suite at a hotel tucked away in the exclusive Mayfair district of London. Their personal butler provided them with all the staples they had listed on their wish list: caviar, chocolates, and champagne.

Coop failed to return Francine's messages. In an effort to be incommunicado, Mercedes turned off her cell and unplugged the phones in the room.

"I've had it with her! She's so controlling, and it's going to feel great to be rid of her," Coop stormed.

"You've been rid of her for over a year—that's what a divorce is for."

"Not Sirena—Francine. I think she's been under the misconception that she's running my life, not just my publicity. I'm against how she's been treating you. It's the same way she acts toward Charlie. The ones who do the work aren't getting the credit. I've had just about enough of Arthur too."

"I'm so glad you weren't thinking about Sirena, were you?"

"No. I'm over her, believe me. There was always some part of her that she withheld from me. I couldn't figure it out, but we were never a perfect fit. We might have outwardly looked like we were a match but not always when we were alone. Not like the two of us," Coop said. He pulled Mercedes closer to him, and her scent and touch made his body stir.

"Do you think she's always been with Amelia?" Mercedes asked, leaning her head against his.

"I guess so, but who knows? I caught them together on the last day in Sacramento on the movie shoot. Sirena said she didn't feel well at the wrap party and went back to the house. Amelia left to keep her company. I felt bad about staying there hanging with everyone, so I cut out a little later."

Mercedes gently pressed her lips to his. He talked through her barrage of light kisses, and then she settled back to listen.

"I went upstairs and didn't find Sirena. When I got to Amelia's room, the door was closed, but I could hear them. It took way too long for them to open the locked door. I know what it's like to try to get away with that kind of thing, I'm sorry to say." Coop stared, looking forward as if imagining the scene. "When they finally opened the door, Amelia was flushed and nervous, but Sirena appeared calm. You can never trust an actor. Sirena started to say how her head was killing her and Amelia had some pills in her room. The bed was a wreck, and Sirena's makeup was less than her usual perfect; I just knew."

"So that's why you left her?" Mercedes asked. "Neither of you ever said what happened. Every one of your *so-called* friends spoke to the media, but the two of you never gave interviews."

"Sirena told me that night she didn't mind that we could never have kids. It was helpful to her career to be married to a big star. She said she loved only Amelia."

"What was Amelia doing this whole time?"

"Blubbering that she was sorry. Amelia claimed she never wanted to hurt anybody."

"Sirena threatened to go public with our secrets if I said anything to the press about Amelia. She said it would hurt her film career—that leading ladies aren't usually outed as lesbians. The public won't buy them in romantic roles with male costars anymore."

Mercedes pulled Coop's face close to hers. "So there are more secrets? What else are you hiding?"

"I've wanted to tell you this. If we're going to have a future, you've got to know the truth."

"Just tell me," Mercedes said softly, dreading his answer. She closed her eyes and listened.

Coop held his breath for a few seconds and then exhaled loudly. "I'm the reason Sirena and I couldn't have kids. I've got a genetic disorder."

"Is it life threatening?" Mercedes held his face in her hands and looked into his eyes. "You can tell me the truth. I can take it."

The corners of Coop's lips lifted. "We're all going to die one day, but I don't expect to croak from Kleinfelter's syndrome. I was born with an extra X chromosome, a rare birth defect that left me infertile with walnuts for balls."

"The rest of you works just fine. I thought they were part of your boyish charm," Mercedes said, running her hands across his crotch.

"How does it sound for the world's sexiest man to be sterile? I used to have learning problems and wasn't very coordinated. At first my mom thought I was dyslexic, but they discovered the birth defect through blood tests. Participating in sports was a nightmare. And can you imagine—my dad was a coach. I've been taking testosterone shots for years."

"So you don't really have allergies? That's one good thing, wouldn't you say?" she joked, gently kissing his neck. "I'm just glad to have *you*. You're what I want in life."

Filled with relief and longing, they kissed deeply, wrapped in each other's warmth. Coop felt at home in a way he never had before.

"If you want kids, we can adopt," he said.

"Hey, you haven't popped the big question yet. Ask me when it's all about us—only us, and then I'll answer you."

"Okay, but how about a professional marriage for now? I've been talking to Silverlake Pictures about setting up my own production company on the lot. They'll get a first-look option on my films. I put in one condition that's a deal-breaker, but I think they'll go for the whole package."

"What is it?"

"You're it: that they pick you up as my new publicist on all my films. How about your taking Francine's spot? You could work exclusively with Lion's Lair Productions, my new company."

"My first client: a Hollywood superstar. You're on!" Mercedes said and sealed the deal with a probing, loving kiss. "And I say yes to both of your proposals!"

Coop beamed his most genuine and dazzling smile. "Award or no award, I'd say I'm the biggest winner in the galaxy!"

F ROM HIS PERCH IN THE CORNER office on the nineteenth floor, Arthur looked at the red blanket of coral trees below. The months after the Movie Constellation Awards hadn't allowed for a respite in the workflow. With thirty pictures opening each year, marketing constantly faced the challenge of a new product introduction—one that had a limited "shelf life" of a few weeks in theaters.

I should have gotten a huge bonus. Manny acts like every penny is his own that he can't part with. He's the chairman, not the owner of the studio, Arthur thought.

Arthur's secretary buzzed. "Mr. Silverstein is on line one."

"Manny, my man, what's shakin'? Hopefully not the Hollywood sign." Silence—no laughter on the other end of the line. "What ... quakes aren't funny these days?"

"Arthur, there's no easy way to say this; you've got to pack up your stuff and vacate your office now. We'll send your things over later. Jamaal's on his way to escort you out of the building."

"Is this some kind of joke? It's not April Fool's Day," Arthur said with a rough laugh.

"No joke, you're just not cutting it. *Big House, Little Lady* was a hit, but the rest of the slate didn't meet box office projections."

Arthur felt his blood surge in his temples. "Oh, there are no bad movies, just bad marketing campaigns. Is that it?"

"No, you're becoming a liability. We dodged the bullet with that sex thing with Gabe where there wasn't any solid proof of misconduct. Luckily, he dropped the charges when he landed another job right away, so it didn't cost us anything. But you're a ticking time bomb. Arthur, I might be on the top floor of this building, but I hear what's going on below. Some of the stars and filmmakers won't work with you anymore, particularly the females."

"That cock-sucker Coop! Did he have something to do with this?"

"Arthur, you're not getting it. You've had a good run, but it's over. Times have changed, and you can't treat women the way you have for years. It has finally bitten you in the ass, and there have been rumblings about formal complaints. Legal will get in touch with you for your exit interview."

"No, Manny, you'll be hearing from my pit-bull, hard-ass lawyer. I treat those bitches just fine. Get ready for the fight of your life."

"Hang on while I check my pockets. Oh yeah, they're still deeper than yours."

"And who's the lucky guy who's going to take over my job at this shit hole of a studio? Bet you've already lined up my replacement," Arthur said, banging his fist on his desk.

"Wrong again! There's no guy."

Jamaal stood at the door and knocked lightly on the jam. "Sorry, Arthur, you've got to go. We'll lock your office, and then your personal items will be returned to you."

Arthur stuffed into his briefcase a few of the silver-framed photos of himself with movie stars, usually with his arms clinched around the females.

"Hate to tell you, the pictures are yours, but the studio owns the frames," Jamaal said.

"You sorry SOB." He grabbed the photo of Teeni and tucked it under his arm. "My wife bought this crystal frame in Paris, in case you're wondering."

"Only following the rules. Don't make this any harder than it is," Jamaal said calmly.

Arthur straightened his tie and turned to Jamaal. "No problem. I just signed a new five-year deal. I'll be on vacation at my beach home in Hawaii for the next few years while you assholes are working like slaves." Arthur slammed his office door so hard that the windows rattled.

After you," Jamaal said coolly. "We'll keep toting those celluloid bales, suh."

3 2
CHARLIE

A FEW WEEKS LATER, CHARLIE RETURNED to the Silverlake Pictures tower. From her office window, she marveled at the coral trees far below.

"So we'll go with the Southwestern motif, right?" the interior designer asked her, gathering fabric swatches into a neat pile.

"Karen, make it more cowgirl than cowboy," Charlie answered and thumbed through the renderings scattered across her desk.

"To be honest, that color palette might be a bit passé."

"If it was good enough for the biggest director in the world, Steven Spielberg, it's good enough for me," Charlie said.

"I think we should be able to pull it off for about twenty," Karen said.

"Twenty people won't fit in here for a meeting. Maximum is ten, wouldn't you say?"

"Twenty thousand dollars. That's the budget to redecorate your office. We should be able to squeeze in a few pieces of original folk art." Karen consulted her spreadsheet.

Charlie leaned back in the leather desk chair. "I don't want this monstrous desk. A round table—something marble or sandstone—will work better for me. It's much more inclusive."

Karen scribbled a large circle over the rectangle on the space plan. "Okay, Ms. Wallach. I'll get right on it and will report back to you when I've got some stone selections for you."

"Oh, you can call me Charlie. Sounds like a plan. Thanks, Karen."

Charlie's interoffice line buzzed. "Tony Everett, your ten o'clock, is here," Amy announced.

"Great. Please ask her in."

Charlie walked to the door to escort Karen out of the office. A tall woman with a complexion and voice like aged cognac greeted Charlie with a confident handshake.

"Have a seat." Charlie joined her on the couch across from the desk. "I am so glad you're finally here. We've been playing catch-up ever since Gabe returned to his former employer who offered him a big promotion after the experience he gained in Hollywood."

"I plan on staying at Silverlake for a long time! My studio let me leave a few days after I gave notice, so I'm thrilled it worked out for both of us," Tony said.

"Great! I know you've been in the business a few years, but I want to pass along something I was told early on when I started working in the motion picture industry."

Tony reached to open her briefcase to get her digital tablet.

Charlie put her hand on the case. "You don't need to jot this down. After I got my first thank-you present from a big star, I thought I'd really made it. Then my boss gave me this advice: If they call you, it's not personal; if they don't call you, it's not personal."

Tony laughed and then nodded her head yes.

"You're great pals during the making and marketing of a film. But when it's over, don't expect to be sipping martinis with them all the time."

"I hear you," Tony agreed.

Amy knocked softly and entered the office, struggling to deliver a massive floral arrangement that she put on the coffee table. Charlie dug through the riot of color and retrieved the card, which she read aloud: "Charlie, congrats, Ms. President of Marketing at Silverlake Pictures! I think this is the beginning of an awesome friendship. — Coop."

She turned to Tony and said somberly, "And there's one more Golden Rule of Hollywood: It's not enough to succeed; your competition must fail!"

"That's pretty cold," Tony muttered, her smile beginning to lose its bloom.

Charlie snapped off an expectant red rosebud and tucked it into her jacket lapel. "But that's their rule and not mine—and rules, just like the glass ceiling, are meant to be broken."

The End

ACKNOWLEDGMENTS

The road to *Red Carpet Rivals* began when I lived in Los Angeles with my husband who was in the fast lane of the movie business. The incidents and characters in the novel sprang from my imagination, but I strived to paint a vivid picture of the "reel" Hollywood. I revealed the unpredictable and glamorous world of the motion picture industry from the viewpoint of an insider who attended countless awards ceremonies.

Just as moviemaking is a collaborative effort, it takes a team to produce a book. Many thanks to Victory Editing for proofing and to Kimberly Martin, Jason Orr and Stephanie Anderson of Jera Publishing for book production. The cover concept was created by BAK LOT Press.

I appreciate the feedback from early readers, including Judith Barnes, Robbi Carrier, Dallas Duncan Franklin, T.W. Lawrence, Laura Levy, Terry Spector, Joanne Truffelman, and Carolyn Lee Wills. *Merci* to Mark and Veronique for checking the French text. Many thanks to Mike Rose and Bill James for their thoughtful comments. Professor Tony Grooms, Dr. Robert Hill, and Dr. Greg Johnson at Kennesaw State University were very helpful in this journey.

Loads of "Big Book Love" to my writer pals across the country who were generous with their advice and encouragement, including many Kathy L. Murphy's Pulpwood Queen's Book Club authors. A warm shout-out to the readers of my first book, *Shelter from the Texas Heat*. You opened your hearts and homes by attending book clubs and exchanging ideas.

As always, my appreciation goes to my glamorous mother, Polly—my best publicist and supporter!

My apricot poodle, GiGi, often waited to play until I could take a break. Sometimes her paws hit the keyboard to get my attention, but I assure you that the content in this book is all mine!

I hope you enjoyed the trip to Hollywood on the pages of *Red Carpet Rivals*. Have "your people" contact "my people" on social media and at literary events! I'd love to hear from you, and I am touched by the kindness of readers.

ABOUT THE AUTHOR

Bobbi Kornblit's award-winning novel, *Shelter from the Texas Heat,* was set in the Lone Star State where she was born and raised. Like her debut work, this highly anticipated second novel revolves around intriguing relationships of characters with secrets and goals, this time set in the exciting world of Hollywood from the 1980s to the present.

In *Red Carpet Rivals,* Bobbi writes from personal experience as the wife of a top movie executive, the late Si Kornblit. Together with her husband, she appeared on numerous red carpets.

Bobbi attended UCLA, earned her BA degree from The University of Texas at Austin, and holds a Master of Arts degree in Professional Writing from Kennesaw State University. She lived in Los Angeles for many years working in advertising and is now a resident of Atlanta. A former journalist, she currently instructs writing at several universities and is involved with the vibrant film industry and literary groups in Atlanta.

Bobbi Kornblit is a frequent speaker at literary festivals and book clubs. She enjoys sharing ideas with reading groups in person and online.

Please visit her at:
www.RedCarpetRivals.com

MORE FICTION BY BOBBI KORNBLIT

Shelter from the Texas Heat

Compared in reviews to *The Help* and *Divine Secrets of the Ya-Ya Sisterhood*, the award-winning novel by Bobbi Kornblit is about holding onto secrets and the power of friendship to release them.

Through laughter and tears, *Shelter from the Texas Heat* tells the story of three generations of women from the Kennedy "Camelot Years" in the 1960s to the present. From funny, turned disastrous moments at a glamorous birthday party, to the painful memories of a Holocaust survivor, *Shelter from the Texas Heat* takes the reader on an emotional roller coaster ride that even includes a stop at the State Fair of Texas.

Honors:
Best Book Women's Fiction: NABE Pinnacle Book Achievement Award
Best Book Multicultural Fiction: Indie Excellence Award
American Library Association: *Booklist Online* "50 Years, 50 Books [about JKF]"
Kathy L. Murphy's Pulpwood Queen's Book Club Recommended Selection

www.ShelterFromTheTexasHeat.com

Red Carpet
Rivals

DISCUSSION QUESTIONS

1. Both Coop and Sirena kept secrets. How did these private matters affect their lives?

2. Are modern movie stars different from the cinema greats of the past such as Audrey Hepburn, Cary Grant, and Vivien Leigh?

3. What were the goals of the main characters and did they achieve them?

4. Is there a glass ceiling in many businesses? Where have women excelled in management?

5. Have you ever been aware of sexual harassment in the workplace? How can it be combatted?

6. Many motion pictures are adaptations of novels. Who would you cast as Coop, Sirena, Francine, and Charlie?

7. The movie industry is known for its awards ceremonies. Which ones contribute to the success of films?

8. If you were to receive a Hollywood award, your statuette would be for Best _____.

Red Carpet
Rivals